SIPPING WHISKY

By George R. White

North America & international
toll-free: 1 888 232 4444 (USA & Canada)
phone: 250 383 6864 • fax: 250 383 6804 • email: info@trafford.com

The United Kingdom & Europe
phone: +44 (0)1865 487 395 • local rate: 0845 230 9601
facsimile: +44 (0)1865 481 507 • email: info.uk@trafford.com

10 9 8 7 6 5 4 3 2 1

This is a fictitious story of a boy that was born illegally during prohibition and protected from Social Services by most all he came into contact with. Around the age of seven he laid eyes on the first child he had ever seen and became her guardian through prohibition, depression, Second World War the golden years and the jaws of an alligator. At the end of prohibition and the death of the mid wife that had delivered him he learned he had a brother and set out with the little girl, a wagon and a dog to find him.

In Appreciation Of

My daughter Rhonda who with bridled patience guided me through the pit falls of computerization

My friends Gord and Audrey Boyd for their continued interest and suggestions

My wife Madeline for her encouragement and ability to spell

Table of Contents

The Twenties

January the seventeenth- nineteen twenty was my lucky day. On the way to the railroad siding where I sold my home brew to the men who rode the rails in search of employment. I came across a Washington Post news paper with a headline that declared prohibition of alcoholic beverages had been in force for twenty four hours. That meant there would be a greater demand for my produce and more money for me.

National prohibition of alcohol was the catalyst that brought about the glamorization of all the things it was meant to suppress and it came into vogue on January 16, 1920. Drunkenness, gang wars, extortion, bribery, rape, murder, prostitution, bootlegged booze; speak easies and the likes of Al Capone. They all prospered under prohibition. For thirteen years young men and women grew up admiring gangsters and wishing to follow in their foot steps. While all this was going on in most of the big cities of America. In the back woods where the little stills operated, rarities like Jack occurred and survived oblivious to the carnage around them and the world beyond their realm.

I had been making sipping whisky the way my dad taught me since I climbed down off his knee. My maw taught me to read and I read everything I could get my hands on from news papers to cereal boxes. I discovered the store in town would sell me an old dog eared book for three cents and if I kept it in half decent shape they would buy it back for a penny. Life was good until my parents died from drinking a poison home made booze, from a friend's still. This would never have happened at my dads still. He used only the proper material in his still and the produce in his sipping whisky. I was the only person that knew his recipe and where the still was so I carried on the business the way dad had taught me. Up and down the line I was referred to as the old man. I accepted that as a title since I was younger than anyone I did business with but my blond hair bleached by the sun appeared almost white and my face was wrinkled and aged. That was probably due to the heat and fumes from the still. Bathing wasn't my large suit either! The railway track was about a mile from my still and half that distance was huge prickly thorn bushes. I always carried a back pack for my bottles along with a walking stick. Since I always took a different route it came in handy for pushing branches out of my way ore beating off what ever needed beating. That along with a big body and a friendly countenance served me well with my type of customer. If the revenuers came looking for me it would probably be as an old man. Fate had more surprises in store for me and the next one came in the shape of a black man who would be my friend for life. His name was Sickle and he loved dancing even more than making whisky.

Sickle

Sickle was a phenomenon that entered my life for no apparent reason and at a time when any abuse of black people was punishable by little more than a slap on the wrist. There was a clearing just far enough from the tracks to be off the railroad property. This was where the rail riders camped while they waited to catch a train. One evening I could hear a lot of racket coming from that direction. It sounded like a party and an opportunity to sell some whisky. When I arrived there were a half a dozen men in a circle around a black man. The black guy had a fancy pair of black and white tap shoes tied together and hung around his neck. The other men were chanting dance nigger dance and whipping his bare feet with switches.

When they saw me they hollered "grab a switch and join the party." "You guys look a little dry to me" I said. "For a small price my elixir could cure that."

"We ain't got no money they said."

"Well I'll give ya a jug for the nigger"

I replied. "I need some one to gather wood for my still."

"It's a deal" they said in unison.

Then I whispered "you stay close behind me boy" and we left the party as inconspicuously as possible while they argued over who owned the jug.

When we got back to the still I asked him. "What the hell were you doing there?"

"I was going to New York City to dance on Broadway" he told me.

"I've seen you dance in town, you're pretty good but have you got any money" I asked?

"No" he said "but I got my shoes and a coat and a sandwich."

"Those guys would eat your sandwich and put on your coat and shoes. Then they'd tie you to the back of the train and run you to New York City. You had better find another way to get to New York. In the meantime you owe me for a jug of whisky. So get fetching some fire wood." Sickle stayed with me through prohibition and learned to make the brew. He even improved it with some herbs his mother suggested. Now it was not only good to drink but killed stomach worms and took the itch out of poison ivy. Sickle was about five and a half feet tall, very black and slim. He never stopped smiling or dancing no mater what he was doing. Whether he was gathering wood, mixing the brew or telling you a story that was were usually about his momma. Those feet of his were magic and he was as agile as a cat. His feet would throw the stick in the air and he would catch it in his arms. He never ran in straight line either, because as he put it his feet thought that was boring.

The Peach

Every couple of days a freight train would pull off the track onto the siding to let the express train through. I could tell by the whistle blasts when they did. Then I would go down to the track and sell my sipping whisky to the rail riders. On this particular night a box car opened and four guys appeared in the opening. Two of them bought a bottle for a quarter.

A third guy said "I got no money but I'll give you a fresh Georgia peach for one of those."

"It's a deal" I said handing him the bottle and drooling at the thought of a fresh ripe peach. "There it is" he said throwing a woman out of the car and closing the opening. "We got her fresh out of Savannah." She was wearing a fur coat that more than likely saved her from some bruises and scrapes from her fall. Lying there on the ground with all that fur around her she looked more like road kill than anything else. A sip of my elixir though put new life into this carcass, as I knew it could. She also appeared to be about four months pregnant according to the old Crone. She just seemed to materialize at times like this and take charge of the situation. I was more than grateful for her presence since my inadequacy with women was nothing short of total frustration. I assumed she had been some gangster's girl friend and he gave her a train ride to celebrate when he discovered she was pregnant. The gratitude of the other passengers lasted only as far the first stop. With the help of Sickle we got her back to camp. When the Old Crone got her cleaned up she proved to be a mid aged raven haired brown eyed beauty with a radiant light creamy brown complexion to her skin. She also proved to have a capacity for my elixir.

She refused to tell us anything about herself not even her name. That caused her to be referred to as Peaches or the Peach as conversation required. Her degradation was such that she no longer had any respect for her mind or body. The old man and her got along just fine since they didn't have to talk they would just raise their glasses in a toast until they passed out. Her sole ambition was to deliver her child and do what she could for it. Then leave this world behind.

Jacks Arrival

Jack was the fruit of the over ripe Georgia peach that I was tricked into buying for a dram of whisky. Jack had likely been the progeny of a Georgia gangster then given along with his mother to the many rail riders heading north looking for work. Word down the line was that the old mans sipping whisky was the balm that fended off the cold and smoothed out the ride.

The Georgia peach serviced many of the men that sought the whisky but she more often received a beating than a coin. Then the old mans whisky helped kill the pain and numb the mind. She had been given to him all ready swelling with the burden in her belly and resigned to fulfilling her obligation as a woman. Then she would accept her retribution in heaven or hell as fate decreed.

The Peach and the old man were both in a stupor when Jack came into the world and recalled very little of what had happened. The only witness to the event was the old Crone and she wouldn't even acknowledge her presence. She was the basis of most of the folk lore in those parts and it was said her only desire was to die in the arms of Satan and reign as a queen in Hades. This was far from the truth for in her cold and calculating manner she was the Samaritan of this shadowy wilderness and you should hold your tongue when you passed by for the wind told her every thing. One of the tales told of the Crone was that she had cursed the Peach and her babies were turned into frogs and hopped down to the river at birth. You could hear them at night begging her to lift the curse. Another one claimed that an Evangelist Minister had come to lift the curse. But folded his tent that same night and fled north hoping to outrun the baby's cries. The Old Crone saw to it that the Peach fed Jack for almost three years. But when her milk dried up the Peach felt that her only purpose for living was gone. She considered herself of no further use and eventually wandered off to find the Grim Reaper in hope of some thing better in the here after. According to the rumors she only made it to the next town. There was an article in the paper of an unknown woman's body being found near the rail road but no description. Jack missed her but other than feeding the only affection he received came from the Crone and Sickle. On occasion the old man would chuck him under the chin and say, maybe we can make a brewer out of you.

His mother's fur coat was used as his blanket and when the collar came off he wore it across his shoulder like a cape. That along with the peak cap the old man gave him could account for stories of a creature that walked upright and disappeared every time it found a bottle. Some believed it could dive into the bottle and run off with it through the brush. This too was credited to the Crone.

Jacks Eden

From that day on Jack was allowed to wander as he pleased since the old man was either selling booze or drinking it and was oblivious of the world around him. Jacks wanderings took him to the Crone's shanty one day. It was pretty run down but it had an out house and a little barn with chickens and rabbits and a boney jersey cow along with some hay and straw. Jack had found Eden. Then he saw that sow just lying there while those little piglets fed. He knew right away this was a momma. He also noticed they were all naked. So he took off the overalls Sickles mom had made for him then jumped right in and found a teat for him self. He was treated no differently than livestock by the old Crone who was in fear of being branded a kidnapper and arrested or "even" worse a witch and turned on by the locals. In their fear they were capable of unbelievable cruelty. He was fed and bedded with the rest of the animals and that was fine by Jack. The animals played with him and at night they huddled together to keep warm. That gave rise to another rumor that one of her weanlings was not even a piglet but something she had turned into a sort of gnome.

Most any other creature would have died gladly under Jacks yoke. But Jack thrived. He grew strong and feared nothing neither dead nor alive. But of course he hadn't seen a girl yet! He wasn't handsome but his features were strong and friendly. His hair was chestnut brown and straight and his shoulders broad. Young as he was it was obvious he had the stature to develop into a fine looking man. Jack never questioned whether beauty was in the eye of the beholder or the one beheld. But when the Crone approached with her pail of slops the pigs weren't the only ones that got excited. But whether the beauty was in the Crone or the pail of slops was never determined by those in the barn. To the Crone it was all a ruse to keep her and the minister out of jail. The slops were actually the contents of broken crates from the depot at the railroad station and wind falls from a local orchard. The mash after distilling was mixed in to keep it from exposing the old mans still.

Some time around the age of five the old man a confident of the old Crone started taking Jack fishing with him. He taught him how to catch catfish and clams and crayfish and each night he would share the catch with Jack. It was the closest Jack had ever come to friendliness or even acceptance What Jack didn't eat raw right there in the boat he would give to the Crone who would at times give him some cooked fish and even allow him to eat at the table with her. As he grew older he was allowed to stay in the house as long as he wished but he preferred the barn. Out there it was warmer and he didn't feel obligated to the other tenants for anything. They mutually shared their warmth and acceptance and asked for no more. The piglets were eventually weaned along with Jack. When they were taken away Jack found it lonely in the barn and moved closer to the sow but he was soon to learn he was no longer welcome. Then the Crone took him into the house and taught him to disappear when strangers came near. He eventually became quite adept at it.

It was around this time that a bank robbery took place in a town about ten miles north of the Crones shanty and would herald the final chapter of her life, as her friends knew it. Due to her calling as mid wife to the poor people in this area the Crone had become well acquainted with the misery and injustice that governed their lives. The thieves realized that the police would have no problem picking up their trail. When their car started acting up they decided to stash the money. When the car stopped one of them jumped out and hid the money under a rock not realizing the Crone was standing not fifty feet away. She stayed where she was until the police had gone by. She was well aware that they were as corrupt as the men they were chasing. She also knew that the bank owner would claim they took twice what they did and that he and the mayor had teamed up to bilk the people of their property.

With this money she would buy the properties in danger of foreclosure. The deeds were sold to the Eternal Light church to avoid taxes. This church was led by the Reverent Richard Blessing, a trust worthy man who would call for an audit of the bank and the Mayor. Once that had been done the people would get their properties returned with a paid up mortgage. The fact that the police shot it out with the thieves and killed them all made the plan even safer. The Crone saw too it that her plans had all been initiated and the banker and Mayor had been indicted. When all these maters were settled she felt ready to shed this life. Her only regret would be leaving Jack but she had taught him as much and as well as she could. She had spoken to the old man about him and given him the paper with what in formation she dared. Any more would have endangered others. It would be left to the old man to carry on his education. When she passed away as the old man and the reverend knew she would. The reverent claimed her and buried her in an unmarked grave as she had requested. In a nice little town that had recently been renamed Blessing.

New Home

A few days before the Crone died the old man took Jack to his shanty and reintroduced him to his friend and side kick Sickle who worked his still and made their so called sipping whisky. Sickle was usually under the influence of his own creation but this day he had stayed sober. He and Jack were friends from the first hand shake. Sickle told him and the old man that there were men out there looking to buy their sipping whisky for big money. Jack had no idea what big money was and even though he pictured in his mind a penny as big as him self. He couldn't imagine what to do with it. But if it made Sickle and the old man happy it was all right with him. They celebrated their new friendship that night. They had a party and ate store bought bread and cheese and drank sipping whisky. Sickle did a crazy dance for them. Jack not knowing how to dance and never having been to a party before, just jumped around banging two sticks together. The old man just sat in his chair rocking and laughing. The party ended for Jack behind the outhouse where he puked until he passed out. That would be his first and last taste of hard liquor. Although in time he did eventually develop a considerable capacity for beer. It took two days of head ache puking and diarrhea to clean Jack out. But it was a lesson he never forgot. Still they had such a good time and no one knew when Jack was born so they decided to declare it Jacks birthday and celebrated it every year after that. This was December the fifth and prohibition would end on Jacks birthday in nineteen thirty three. As a birthday present the old man gave him a Swiss army pen knife. It would give Jack many hours of contentment finding ways to use the many utensils on it and he never went any where with out it. As his gift Sickle showed him how to make a whistle with it from a piece of bamboo and how to change the tone by making more holes to put his fingers over.

Eventually the old Crone that had been Jack's mentor since his birth went to meet Satan and sit on the throne beside him, as most people thought. But Jack and the old man knew about the big heart that beat behind the shabby but clean cloths the old woman wore. She was no beauty with her broad flat nose that looked like a rotten apple had been crushed on the stern pock marked face that only Jack could soften. Her back was bent from a kick by that old jersey cow. She wore a dress that reached about six inches below her knees and rubber boots from there on down. An old fedora hid her face from most people. Others were inclined to look away most of the time for fear of the evil eye. Jack loved her and though words were never spoken the feeling was mutual

She left a letter with the old man. It was to be given to Jack when he was old enough to read and under stand what it meant. But fate determined that the revenuers not the old man would decide when he was old enough. This revelation would come to Jack when he had more responsibility than any youngster should have to bear. The journey he would eventually embark upon was beyond his comprehension. Jack was a pupil of nature. Paths, flora and water all said something to Jack, but once he stepped out of the woods he would have to learn another language. Roads, side walks, traffic and crowds were not in Jack vocabulary.

The Company

The three friends decided to form a company as equal partners and the old man would keep a record of their expenses loses and profits. Then once a week they would divide the profits leaving one forth for capital. Sickles a share would be given to his mother since he wasn't married, to dole out as she saw fit. This arrangement was okay with him since he realized he would just flaunt it around town until people wondered where it came from. Jacks share was put in a money belt the old man had made from the skin of a rattle snake he had killed. It was big enough to go around Jack twice and be adjusted as he grew. The belt would give Jack security if he had to leave in a hurry. As it is an unwritten law that where the whisky runners went the revenuers followed. Sickle was the brew master and some kind of sewer of fine alcohol. The Crone had often used his elixir as a cure for the ague but would never disclose its source.

Jacks job was to collect bottles to hold their product and the old man had made him a wagon to put them in. One of his sources was the old Crone's property now that she was gone and he would make it his last stop of the day. That is until the day he discovered a man and a little girl in there cleaning the place up. He hadn't noticed the little girl until he asked the man not to break those jars. Then he couldn't take his eyes off of her! He had never seen one before but then, he had never seen any children not even himself. All though he had seen a creature looking at him out of the pond a couple of times but it was messy dirty looking thing and Jack figured it to be something the old Crone had whipped up. It was safer not to look at such a thing lest it drag him into the water with it. Jack knew it would because one day he reached out to touch the water and a hand came out to grab his. Jack leaped away in time to avoid it but he wouldn't try that again.

This critter was clean and had shiny yellow hair with a bow in the back to hold it together. It wore a shirt that came right down to its knees and was tied in the middle with a pretty rope. When it bent over it had flowers on its bum and shiny black shoes. Jack wasn't afraid of it though. It only came up to his chest and as long as it wasn't poison or prickly or sticky he could handle it.

"Maybe I had better help you with those bottles" the man said as he picked up a couple and walked over to put them in his wagon. "What do you want them for" he asked?

But Jack couldn't answer because the critter was trying to get in his wagon. In one brief terrifying moment Jack had learned fear and frustration and could think of nothing better to do than grab his wagon and run away. When he pulled the wagon away the little girl fell over and began to cry. That only made Jack run faster and when he got out of sight in the woods he sat down on a stump. He felt sorry he had hurt the little creature and was haunted by the strange noise it made. It looked almost like a little person. He thought, it's probably sticky or prickly or it wouldn't have all those flowers stuck to its bum. But he still wanted one, more than any thing else in the world. Jack didn't know how to cry, in his world if something bothered you, you fought it until it fled or like any sensible animal accepted retreat as the wiser part of valor and did the running.

When he got back to the still he told the old man about the man at the Crones house and the strange creature that tried to get in his wagon.

"Well the old man said you have seen the Siren and heard her call and you can never be the same again."

"Will I die" Jack wanted to know?

"We all die son sooner or later." He said. "But whether we end up at the Pearly Gates or by the River Styx our last thought will probably be of the Siren."

All this information was more than Jacks brain could absorb at one time. The only thing he could retain was that he would remember the Siren for the rest of his life.

"I had best go and see this man and determine whether or not his presence will have any effect on our company" said the old man.

So it was that the old man went to meet the stranger. He didn't take Jack with him because he needed to probe the man for information and he wasn't sure he wanted him to know that he and Jack were acquainted. At least till he knew more about him!

The man introduced himself as Hector Craig and said "just call me Hec my friends do."

Then he invited him in to have a cup of tea.

The old man claimed to be Melvin Upwrite. But said "just call me old man or Mel if old man doesn't sit right with you." They talked for along time and Hec told him he had been a social worker and a teacher. But since prohibition had lost them the tax on liquor a lot of people had lost their jobs including him. Then he became very morose and said "the bank took my house and my wife ran off with a revenuer.

"Now" he said "the social workers say they are going to take my daughter unless I have a place to live. So I bought this house at a government auction for seventy five dollar. I have two weeks to make my note good."

"I'll drop by in a few days to see how you're making out" the old man said. He then waved goodbye and stepped into the woods and was out of sight. To his surprise Jack was standing there watching the little girl and so mesmerized he hadn't even noticed the old man looking at him.

"Next time we come he said I'll introduce you. But first you have to learn something about girls."

"Did you see it" Jack asked? "Is it poison?"

"You don't call her an it she's a she or a her no hers a she I mean she's a girl and girls are females. "Damn" he said "We'll talk about this later. Right now we have to get those bottles filled. There is going to be a train through in about an hour."

A couple of days later some men came to see the old man. They were big rough looking men in pretty fancy cloths for roaming around the woods. What they proposed was that the old man should keep his little still operating but they would finance a bigger one farther back in the bush. He could turn out a few at his little still for the rail riders and the revenuers to find if they came around. .But the bulk of his business would be done at the big still and they would pick it up at regular intervals. That was when the money really started coming in.

The next day Jack and the old man went to see Hec and the little girl.

On the way Jack ask the old man. "Why did I have to wash my face?"

"Because you want to look nice for the little girl don't you?"

"I don't know and you didn't tell me about hers and she's and you didn't say if it was poison."

"You're calling it an it again. Now see what you done you got me calling it an it and it ain't poison. Just shut up I'm trying to think and don't forget the bottles."

When they got to the old crones house the man and the little girl were sitting on the steps. The little girl jumped up as soon as she saw them and ran over shouting "wagon- wagon!"

Jack stepped in her road and she kicked him in the shins. That was all it took Jack was totally smitten.

He just looked at the old man and asked "are you sure it ain't poison?"

But it didn't matter anymore Jack couldn't have been more of a slave if he had been in shackles. She climbed in his wagon and yelled giddy up and he pulled her around until they left. While Jack was acting like a draft horse for Peggy Sue the old man bought Hecs note for the house and offered him a job with the company to take care of the new still. Ordinarily Hec would have nothing to do with breaking the law. But after all that had happened to him and his daughter he considered this a protest against the government. On top of that he hated revenuers.

Sickle didn't mind the new man joining the company and running the big still. He liked running the little still it gave him more time to talk to the rail riders and he was proud they liked his recipe and was going to use it at the new still. Jack told him about the little girl and the shiny black shoes and the flowers on her bum and her name was Peggy Sue. Jack seemed to say it with reverence. Sickle was amazed at how smitten Jack was. But he didn't make fun of him.

He just smiled and said "I want to be there when you meet a full grown one." Then he told Jack that he had real fancy shoes with white toes and heels and steel taps on the front and back.

Jack asked why he never wore them instead of running around in his bare feet.

Because they are only for dancing if I wore them all the time they would wear out and I couldn't dance the same. But these feet they never wear out. They just get tougher and tougher all the time. God sure knows what he is doing.

Another nice thing about the new still was they didn't have to cut wood. They used coal oil and even had a fan to blow the fumes away. Things were going good for the little company. Jacks belt kept getting thicker. Hec turned out to be a talented brewer and Jack took the filled jugs to different locations for pickup and became quite talented at disguising them. They bought a big friendly dog that howled every time someone came around then would go out and welcome them in. That frustrated any revenuers that might try to sneak up on them.

Jack took the old mans little flat bottomed aluminum boat and under the old mans direction made a wagon out of it that the dog could pull. They put large carriage wheels on it and shafts to keep it from running over the dog. It had a ridgepole with a crank and a camouflage tarp over it. Peggy Sue loved to ride in it and Jack never tired of taking her and the dog on forays even though he always maintained a tight grip on Woofs leash. Jack never gave a thought to the difference in their ages. His life now had a purpose and it was expendable on her behalf. Any situation was a pleasure to Jack as long as they shared it. They often caught frogs and would splash in the water and never fear their reflections because now they knew what they were . They would catch fire flies and put them in a bottle for a lamp and when the old man played his harmonica they would flash off and on to the music. When she got stung by a bee Jack put mud on it the way Sickle had showed him and held her until she stopped crying.

The Learning Years

Peggy Sue always had a book with her full of pictures and the alphabet and numbers up to a hundred. She was constantly singing from her book and Jack would sing along and look at the pictures with her. At times even the dog would join in and Peggy Sue named him Woof. Things went well for the company for a couple of years. Hec would give lessons from the book on how to put the letters together to form words and how to relate the numbers to the bottles or stones.

Sickle dug a hole behind the out house and put a trap door on it. Then they stocked it with canned and bottled goods. They put lots of lye in the out house to put the dogs of the scent if the revenuers came. The old man could hide in there. Jack would come and give their signal when it was safe. Sickle figured he would just out run them. He ran like the wind but never in a straight line and he leaped like a kangaroo so if he wasn't going from side to side he was going up and down. As for the dogs he had some skunks in cages with ropes on them he could pull as he ran by that would throw them out of their cages in a fit of fear and anger. Then they became the dog's problem. Sickle's mother had put a good sum aside and as long as they lived conservatively they should have no problems.

Hec was expected to take a round about route home. In order to protect Peggy Sue he hadn't been exposed to anyone they knew. So he shouldn't be involved. There were rumors circulating, of the abolition of prohibition and a push was ordered on the arrest of the brewers and tax evaders.

The revenuers showed up on the property in June of nineteen thirty three. Woof let out his warning howl and they took a few shots at him. Even though it only took one to make their presence known and his presence scarce. They had dogs with them. But it seemed Woof was not in the mood for company. They took a few shots at the blur that was Sickle but to no avail and the dogs were made useless by the skunks, as they would be for quite a while. The old man high tailed it to his hide away. He had been putting the finishing touches on it for quite a while now and had it quite comfortable. It was on a bit of a knoll so he had no need to worry about being flooded out. It was seven feet long four wide and six deep. He had lined it all around and top and bottom with plywood and had shelves on the one end. The shelves held his strong box with his money and the letter the old crone had left for Jack. There was a twenty by twenty inch opening at the other end wit a tapered plug so the old man could tell if it was in the right position from the inside. Some shag grass on the top covered the outline of the hole and an old hollow tree stump covered his breathing hole. The revenuers blew up the small still and set fire to the old mans house then they pushed the out house over unaware it had landed on the old mans hide out.

Jack and Peggy Sue along with Woof and the cart took the long way to Hecs house. They waited all night and all the next day but he never showed up. That night Jack put Peggy Sue to sleep then leaving Woof to guard her went to see if he could find the old man. When he got to the house it had burnt to the ground. Then he realized the out house was on top of the old mans hide out and with the help of a pole he managed to slide it away from the plug. The old man was very glad he had come back he had been trying to get the plug out but he didn't have the strength to lift the plug and the out house too. The two of them made their way back to Hecs house in the dark. They needed to make some plans for the future of not only themselves but Peggy Sue.

The old man told Jack he heard they had blown up the big still by mistake and someone had been badly injured they were pretty sure he was going to die. It could only be Hec and if they found out who he was they would come after his daughter. The very thought terrified Jack. Peggy Sue had become the very essence of his existence and he would not do without her. Then he said if they came for her they would put him in a reform school and if nothing else he would get an education of sorts. Jack said he had gotten all the education he wanted from Hec. He could count to a hundred and his reading was getting better all the time. On top of that he could sign his name even though he didn't know his last name. He would make one up and he would do it right now. He turned to Peggy Sue what would you like for a last name? She took a big exasperated breath tilted her head to the side and her finger to her mouth then she mused Fluffy, Spot, or-r-r.

That's good the old man said Jack Orr. You can learn to sign it right now. Show me how you sign your name which Jack did then the old man showed him how to add his last name to it He practiced it a couple of time then put the paper in his pocket so he wouldn't forget it. Then they both gave Peggy Sue a big hug for finding such an easy name so fast. Then she marched around the house singing Peggy Sue Orr and Jack Orr and old man Orr and Daddy Orr. There was more to discus with Jack but he figured it would go better after a nights sleep.

In the morning, over a breakfast of cornflakes and toast the old man showed Jack the letter the old crone had entrusted to him.

"To anyone that gives a damn this is Jack or what ever you want to call him. He was born to an old prostitute known only as Peaches he's a twin born half an hour after his brother who was taken away by an evangelist minister at birth and before Jack arrived." signed, Jessica Wade.

There was a PS under her signature. It read the Ministers son had died at birth and in order to have his wife maintain her sanity he was going to replace him with Jacks brother. With out her knowledge! It seemed the right thing to do!

When Jack asked the old man what he was going to do. He said they would have to split up. Since he was a wanted man and if they were caught he'd be charged with kidnapping and sent to jail for life. Then he said I may try to find Sickle I kind of take a shine to his mother. He knew Sickle always wanted to dance on Broudway. He told Jack he could stay where he was until some one found out about them and they came to take them away. Then he said you must keep the little girl clean and nicely dressed but not to nicely or someone may wonder where the money is coming from. If you must buy cloths go to the used or second hand store. I know a lady who could use some extra money and may take you in and possibly register you in school. That would give you some sort of identity. Jack had an aversion to anyone taking care of Peggy Sue but him.

Never the less he said he'd think about it. Still in the back of his mind he wanted very much to find the brother he had just learned he had. But what was best for Peggy Sue had to come first. The old man gave him a post box number he could write to if it was really necessary.

Then he said" it is too risky for me to stay here any longer. She is your responsibility now Jack and I'm sure you'll succeed". Then with a hug for each he joined the other rovers on the train. He knew he would be among friends there.

Jack proceeded to stock the wagon with supplies such as a suit case full of clothes and accessories for Peggy Sue. He threw in a few tools some blankets and a pillow along with several rolls of toilet paper. Since her father couldn't believe how much of it a little girl could use. He put some of her father's cloths in an old carpet bag incase he caught up with them and a big pair of jack-boots. Her father was a slight man while Jack though much younger was taller than most at his age. He was also quite muscular and figured if her father didn't show up he could adjust his cloths to fit himself. Her father to must have been thinking ahead because he had bought a little sewing kit which Jack put in the suit case. Jack agonized most of the night on what to do. First thing in the morning they had some cornflakes and bread and jam. Then they threw some bread and wieners in a basket along with a pot two bowls a couple of spoons and a tin plate for woofs dinner a long with a bottle of water and a couple of cups then headed to the lake for a pick nick and to hide the cart. Once the cart was hidden in the reeds and camouflaged they went to a favorite spot by the lake were they could see the house without being seen.

Her father had picked it out so she and Jack could watch the house in case the social workers came around. Jack didn't like them and it occurred to him that if they could take Peggy Sue away from her father. They could take her away from him. The very concept of it made up his mind. They showed up about mid morning and poked around trying doors and looking in windows. As soon as the social workers were gone he would go to his hiding spot and get his snake skin belt and other money along with a few keep sakes. He would put that along with his letter from the old crone and the post box number in an oil skin pouch and hid it in his secret compartment under the wagon. So far he had been telling Peggy Sue that her father had to work late because of a special order they had. She accepted that because her father had told her many time that if he wasn't around she must stay very close to Jack and do as he said. Now Jack would have to change his story. Jack wasn't accustomed to lying, and deceiving Peggy Sue was painful to him. He would put it off as long as possible. There may be news of her father. "Yet!"

The Journey Begins

Jack was about twelve years old now according to the old mans memory and his entire world had been the woods and swamps. He was truly a denizen of the forest and though he had seen many animals he had never seen a child of his own age or a full grown woman that he could remember. The old man had said that Peggy Sue would be a woman some day. That statement was a constant aggravation to Jack due to his fertile and unfettered imagination. There had been a woman with the Social service people but she had been to far away for him to form any sort of opinion.

Jacks first thought had been to fallow the railroad track like so many of the men looking for work did. The men looking for work were usually fairly nice and helpful. But there was another kind too that Jack wouldn't trust and kept as far from them as possible. He wouldn't want them to even know there was a Peggy Sue. Sickle had told Jack about the points of the compass and how to recognize them. East and west were easy but not much use at night. So they stayed up late one night and Sickle pointed out the north star and how he could always find it by taking a line up the spout of the big dipper. Then Jack wanted to know how come the big dipper was going around the North Star. Sickle tried to explain to him that the stars weren't but the earth was tuning from west to east. Up to this point Jack was thinking Sickle must be the smartest man on earth but now he had to find away to prove to this lunk head that he wasn't going round the North Star. It became a constant argument between them that they enjoyed very much.

Jack had decided they should go north since it seemed everyone he had met was going that way and maybe the evangelist minister was too. The only way the old man could think to tell him to find the minister was to look for signs saying evangelist or prayer meeting and to follow them. He may see something in a news paper too but that was an awful lot of reading for a guy who had to sound out every word. Then he said if you ever hear singing coming out of a tent get right over there. Because you have probably found your man! Then watch his face closely because if he hasn't adopted the boy legally he may lie about it. The old man printed it on a piece of paper so Jack could sound it out then   they parted company. Jack hitched Woof to the cart and they started walking. When Peggy Sue got tired Jack would put her in the cart and he had tied an extra rope to the cart so he could help Woof pull it if necessary. They walked for most of the day because Jack wanted to get as far from those Social Workers as possible. For the first night they camped by the river behind an embankment. With Woof sleeping under the cart and him sleeping with Peggy Sue because she missed her dad and would cry in her sleep sometimes. Then

Jack would pat her and tell her it would be alright and try not to cry himself. But sometimes her tears would create such a pain in his chest he feared it might kill him. Then he would think she would be alone and that was even more terrifying and he would force himself to calm down.

The fallowing morning Jack got Peggy Sue her cornflakes and milk along with apiece of bread and peanut butter. He gave Woof a couple of wieners and had a couple for him self along with a piece of bread and peanut butter. Woof hung over his shoulder all the time he was eating it. Jack gave him a little piece thinking he would go away and leave him alone. That was not to be as he loved it and looked so funny eating it that Peggy Sue laughed and that made Jack feel so good it became part of their daily routine. They were almost out of supplies and Jack realized he would have to go into a store and buy them himself. He had only been in a store once with Sickle and the store keeper stared at him all the time he was there. Now he had to go it alone. The old man had warned him not to let anyone see how much money he had and to use bills of the smallest denomination he needed. He at first considered going in by himself. Then it occurred to him that people were less likely to think anything wrong of a brother and sister shopping together than they would of a boy shopping by himself.

When they entered the store Jack was amazed at the variety of foods there were and the man didn't seem at all concerned about his presence. They even had baskets to put the things in he got two tins of pork and beans a tin of spaghetti. They had fun with spaghetti seeing who could suck in the longest piece and it made Peggy Sue laugh and that made Jack happy and a loaf of bread a quart of milk a bag of dog food ajar of honey some bran flakes ajar of peanut butter. He gave the man a five dollar bill and got change. By that time woof had gotten tired of guarding the cart and appeared at the door. When the man asked if that was his dog he figured he might be in trouble but he said yes. Then the man reached under the counter and brought out a big bone which he gave to woof. Jack was quite pleased with himself for having gotten through what he figured would be a big ordeal. He was glad he had washed his face and Peggy Sue looked nice and neat. As an after thought he bought a bar of Ivory soap since it was the biggest one he could find and he had to wash cloths as well as bodies.

Jacks domestic duties required him to learn more about the female anatomy than he felt he should know. Unfortunately though leaving her to her own devices resulted in rashes and Jacks only known cure for that was axle grease. A remedy he had stumbled on while searching for relief for himself. It got them by until he remembered the yellow bottle of grease that the old man used for every thing. He was sure he would know the bottle when he saw it next time he went into a store. For now Jack just wanted to get into the country side away from people. How would he know whether or not they were Social Workers? They had been traveling for four days now and no one had bothered them. But the dog and the cart attracted attention and that worried Jack. On the fifth day one of the wheels on the cart started sticking. They were passing a golf course when Jack decided he had better grease it. While he was busy Peggy Sue took it upon herself to walk across the street to a pond. When Jack looked to see what Woof was making a fuss about he took off at a run fearing she might go in the water. When he was about twenty feet behind her she started running that is when an alligator about six feet long came out of the water and started after her. Jack didn't hesitate for a second. He leaped on top of the gator wrapping his arms and legs around it and they rolled down the bank together and into the water. Now Jack was in a real dilemma if he let go of the gator it would have him before he could get out of the water and if he hung on to long it would drown him. Fortunately some golfers showed up. One of them had thought to grab a cedar rail on his way and hit the gator over the head with it. The gator bit into the rail that was when Jack let go of him and got out of the water. His first and only thought was to pick up Peggy Sue and assure her every thing was alright. The golfers said that was the bravest thing they had ever seen. Then a young girl his own size but a couple of years his senior stepped up and told him she thought he was the bravest person in the world and snapped his picture. Jack was dumb founded. His face went red a lump formed in his throat and he couldn't breath or shut his mouth. So he did the only thing decorum would allow. "He turned and ran!" Fortunately Woof was still hitched to the cart or he'd have been in the water with Jack. He put Peggy Sue in the cart and left a fast as they could. He turned off the road as soon as possible to avoid being seen any more than he could help. He would fix the wheel when they stopped for the night.

When dusk was coming on Jack stopped at a small clearing in a wood. He lit a small fire and heated up some beans and wiener for supper and fed Woof his dry dog food that was supposed to keep his teeth clean. He tied the ends and one side of the tarp tight to the boat so no strange critters could get in. He slept on the open side. Jack lay there thinking about the girl that had taken his picture. He couldn't help but wondered if Peggy Sue would look like that when she grew up. He finally decided she would be even prettier then fell asleep with a picture of her pixy like face in his mind and the music of the night critters in his ears.

An Allie Is Made

Jack was awakened by the beating of Woofs tail on the side of the cart. When he opened the curtain there was a large man standing there and Woof was trying to take a steak bone out of his hand. The man let go of the bone and greeted Jack with a cheerful good morning. Jack was out of bed and dressed before the man could say another word. Jack looked at the man then said "I know you you're the man that saved me from being drowned by the alligator."

"I saw you light your little fire last night and it seemed a pleasant idea to invite you to breakfast."

"Jack was flabbergasted but Peggy Sue stuck her head out of the cart and said oh" can we have bacon?"

"You bet you can little lady the man said and eggs and toast and jam if you like." "I'll put my best dress on she said but she said to Jack in a whisper I have to pee. Go behind the cart Jack told her and be sure you finished before you pull your pants up.

Ok she said and was gone. She was back in a blink. "Did you do what I said" Jack asked? "Yep" she said but he knew she was lying. But how do you reprimand someone who is so happy? She came out of the cart in her best dress which she had put on backwards and her shiny black shoes on the wrong feet. Then she went over and took the man's hand. Two very happy people led Jack and Woof up to the house that morning. They must have felt quite sure Jack would accept their invitation since the table was set for five.

Then the man introduced himself as Donald Walton and his wife as the boss lady Hilda. Then his gaze turned to the door of another room and the girl who had taken his picture entered. "This is my grand daughter Kelly" he said "and the reason they call them grand daughters."

"I was hoping to meet you again" she said.

Jack was dumb founded but there was no where to run. So he made the most profound statement he could think of, {which sounded like} "uhu!"

Peggy Sue was not so elegant she just wrapped her arms around the girl's legs and said "when I get big I'm going to have a dress like yours too." That broke the ice and Don suggested they all sit down and eat. The girl sat on one side of Jack and Don on the other. Peggy Sue sat between the two women and was enjoying the female company immensely. She hadn't been with a woman since her mother left. Kelly though seemed to be enjoying Jacks misery. Jack had no idea why or how but he seemed to be enjoying his misery too.

Jack sat and talked with Hilda and Don for a long time. They discussed what would happen to them if the Social Workers caught up with them. They showed him a calendar and a map then explained how it might take a year or two traveling the way they were. Only to get to the place where they thought he was then find he had moved to another location. He would have to move much faster in order to catch up with them. They didn't advertise their next location for fear of a bad reception, particularly if they performed with snakes. When they arrived they would put posters all over town and hold a parade. Don being a former executive of the Lodge suggested they stay with them for a couple of days while he asked his lodge brother to help locate the evangelists. When Jack told Peggy Sue what they had asked she became so excited he didn't have the heart to deny her.

The women had been treating her like a doll with bubble baths and hair styling and her cloths on the right way. Not only that but she would get to sleep with Kelly in a big soft bed. Jack insisted on sleeping in the cart. Woof seemed to like the idea of the house but he went with Jack any way. Jack needed time alone to think. Out there in the dark and the quiet of the night he could see things in his own prospectus. In the morning Jack went to the house for breakfast and Peggy Sue bombarded him with all the wonderful things she had been doing. She told him about the dolls, and sleeping with Kelly in the big soft bed. Jack was happy for her and sad too since he couldn't compete with all this luxury she had been exposed to.

After breakfast Kelly took Peggy Sue for a walk while Hilda and Don Explained to Jack that they had gotten word of an evangelist meeting in a little town called Spring Falls about a hundred and fifty miles away. It would be impossible for Jack traveling with Peggy Sue and Woof to get there in less than half a month and they would be long gone by then. They offered to take care of Peggy Sue while he was gone. That would allow Jack to hitch hike or take a bus and get there in a day or so. In the meantime Don would try to get news of her father. Jack agreed with them even though he had no idea what hitch hiking was and had never been on a bus in fact as far as he knew he had never seen a bus. They gave him a road map and put gold stars on where he was and his destination so he could show it to anyone if he was in doubt. They supplied him with a back pack and sleeping bag and a loud of sandwiches. Peggy Sue was torn between Jacks leaving and staying with the Walton's. She made him promise to come back then gave him one of her books that he must return. Woof had to stay behind which categorized him with Peggy Sue .Still they had each other to lean on and woof had never eaten so good. Jack told Don of the money in the cart in case they needed it or something should happen to him. The Walton's cut Jacks hair and introduced him to a bath tub, soap and a mirror for show and tell. Don over saw the event and assured him he would neither be dissolved nor poisoned. Hilda then altered some of Hecs cloths and supplied Jack with a toothbrush and a pocket comb. When they next put him in front of the mirror he had a problem relating to the image in there. It seemed like an awful lot of trouble just to make the mirror look good and it was sort of like looking at the face in the water. But he had no desire to offend his new found friends and he had to admit his head didn't itch anymore. Besides Kelly said he looked handsome and judging by the smile on her face that must be good. More important than any of that Peggy Sue took his hand and said you look really nice Jack and you smell nice too. That would keep him combing his hair for a good while. Don took a pocket watch out of a dresser drawer and after winding it up he handed it to Jack and gave him a quick lesson on telling time. The old man had given him a lesson about telling time and direction with a watch. He knew that if he pointed the little hand at the sun the twelve would point south.

"I'm counting on you to bring this back to me" he said. "It was left to me by my father."

Don accompanied him to town and pointed out the bus stop but didn't want to be seen with him, in case people started asking questions. He explained about the wicket and what to ask the teller then left him on his own and got out of sight. When he got to his house he put the cart in his work shed. Next he packed all the women and Woof in the car, hooked up the trailer and set out to visit his brother. The lodge would keep him up to date on their findings.

The Bus

Jack repeated what Don had told him word for word at the wicket. The teller gave him a ticket for two dollars and told him the bus would leave in an hour she also informed him the bus didn't go off the highway so he would have to walk a few miles to Springfalls. Walking was something very familiar to Jack and he gave it no consideration. Jack bought himself a coke some thing he had never had before but he liked the shape of the bottle. Then he sat as unobtrusively as possible until the bus was ready to leave.

He had notice a girl about the same age as Kelly who seemed to be watching him, and we have already experienced how older women affect Jack. When they entered the bus Jack took a seat at the very back then took out his map to cover his face so he wouldn't look at the girl and she couldn't see him. This ruse was useless the girl eventually pulled the map down from in front of his face and asked if she could look at his map. She didn't wait for an answer but sat down beside him. She looked at his map for a second then said I "know who you are and I see your going to Springfalls." Jack gave her his usual muttered "uhhu." "You're the guy who saved the little girl and wrestled the alligator." "No that wasn't me" he said.

"I'm going to Springfalls too" she said "and it was you. So why are you denying it? You should be proud it's something to brag about. So you must be running away from some one or something." This girl was pretty but she scared the hell out of Jack. Life was a lot easier before he knew about girls. She questioned him all the way to the Springfalls side road.

"Do you think I'd make a good reporter" she asked?

"What's a reporter" Jack asked?

"You know" she replied "one of those people that finds out about things that happen then writes about them"

"I guess they ask a lot of questions" he said.

"Oh yes" she said "they have to get all the facts."

"Papers must be pretty big" Jack said.

When they got off the bus at the Springfalls cut off it was ten o'clock at night and Jack decided he might as well camp right there at the side of the road. When, he told her of his intentions.

She told him "there is no way I'm walking down that road by myself at this time of night. I'll just camp here with you and I'm getting cold already." Jack rolled out his sleeping bag and she needed no invitation. She just climbed right in as if it were her God given right and Jack sat beside it shivering. When his teeth started to chatter!

She said "come on in chicken I won't hurt you." So he did and it didn't hurt. She snuggled up real close and put her arm around him and it was good and warm and she smelled good and his hormones started acting up and he was glad she was behind him. In no time at all they were both asleep.

Jack was awakened by water dripping on his head. When he opened his eyes he was looking up a cow's nose. This was a puzzle he didn't take time to decipher. He sat bolt upright hitting the cow on the nose with his head. The cow took exception to this treatment and ran off kicking and bucking. Fortunately it was checking them out from the other side of a fence or they might have been run over them. Jack had seen these creatures on his walk with Peggy Sue but he had no idea whether or not they were carnivores. But now he knew a good punch on the nose would send them scurrying.

The girl was awake now and she said "you should apologize to that poor critter it was just trying to be friendly. By the way since we have already slept together you should at least know my name. I'm Karley."

"Uhhu" Jack said.

"Is that your name she wanted to know?"

"No" he said "it's Jack."

"Well you're just a barrel of information Jack," she said with frustrated indignation.

"Uhhu" Jack said.

They walked for about an hour with Jack getting the third degree all the way.

Finally she said "you may as well tell me Jack or I'll have to make it all up on my own and I have a great imagination."

Jack very much wanted to tell some one but he wasn't sure she was the right someone. After all she must have told him every thing that had ever happened in the world by now. So why would she keep this a secret? Then he thought it might be alright if I told her a little bit. He remembered the old man telling him if anyone asked he must tell them Peggy Sue was his sister or they would put them in reform school. It was a place with iron bars on its windows and people hit you with sticks if you did anything wrong. The idea of anyone hitting Peggy Sue with anything turned his stomach and made the blood rush to his head. So he told her Peggy Sue was his sister and that was why he tackled the alligator. Now he said he must find his brother because he was older and they could be a family. Jack could see that Karley felt very deeply about his plight. But a big tent suddenly appeared on the horizon and all but the tent was forgotten. They ran all the way to the gate where a man ask them for twenty five cents each. Jack gave him the money then asked if that was the Evangelists tent.

"Hell no" the man said "we threw them out of here a couple of days ago."

"Do you know where they went" Jack asked?

"No" the man said "But the manager might know." The man pointed to the manager's trailer and they headed toward it. When they got there a short stout man in a brown suit coat with yellow stripes was standing in the doorway.

"What can I do for you young folk" he said "are you looking for a job?"

Jokingly Karley said "have you got an alligator, Jack wrestles them."

"Well no" the manager said "but we could get him one."

"She's just kidding" Jack said   "I just want to know if you know where the evangelists went?"

"Have you really wrestled an alligator" the manager asked?

"Yes he did" Karley said "and rescued a little girl too." A sly grin came on the manager's face at her remark and it startled Karley.

"You wait here" he said "I'll ask around. Maybe someone else knows where they're headed. Tilley he called give these young folk something cool to drink will you." In a couple of minutes a bearded lady appeared at the door with two glasses of juice in her hands.

"This will cool you off" she said with a wink. You couldn't tell if she was smiling, the beard covered her mouth so completely. When the manager returned he had a huge man with him that he introduced as Titan the strongest man in the world.

"We just call him Ti" he said. "Anyway Ti says he heard them talking about Swansea and we just happen to be going there in the morning. If you care to give us a hand to pack up we could take you with us. That would save you waiting half the day for a bus. Do you still have your bus ticket?"

"Sure" said Jack taking it out of his pocket. The manager looked at it then gave it back. "It's only one way" he said "so you'll save a bit of money too."

"I have to go" Karley said "my aunt was expecting me yester day. I'm glad I met you Jack and I hope you find your brother."

"Uhhu" Jack said.

"Gabby isn't he" she said as she walked away "and not as gentle as he may seem. He head butted a cow this morning just for looking at him."

The Circus

When she had gone the manager turned to Jack "Ti will show you what to do." Then he said to Ti "Tell Leo to come and see me." Leo was the lion tamer and in charge of all the animals with the circus.

When Leo showed up at the office Max the manager took him inside. They sat down at a table and Tilley poured them a drink.

I've got an idea to expand the show Max told him.

I'm listening Leo said.

The young girl that came in with the lad tells me he wrestled an alligator to save a little girl. Now if you were to go into Harborville that's where his ticket was bought and ask around a bit you may get the whole story. Take some equipment with you in case you want to bring that alligator back.

Jack work through the whole night packing the big tent. He couldn't under stand why he was so tired but the determination to find his brother kept him going. Max told him he had phoned the mayor of Swansea to confirm their appointment and found it had been canceled along with the evangelist due to a tornado warning. So now we are going to Elloree and so are the evangelists. It took most of the night to get to Elloree and when they did the evangelists weren't there. Max claimed they had further to travel than them and so would take longer to get there. It may even take them an extra day to make it. They set about putting up the big tent and when Leo returned he parked the truck on the edge of the parking lot under some trees. Max and Leo spent considerable time in the office discussing Leo's business in Harborville.

Max finally called Jack into the office and told him he might better sit down. They told him that Leo had made a trip to Harborville to get the special ropes they needed for the trapeze and had heard people talking of the boy who had saved his sister from an alligator. They told him that the social services had his sister and had put her in the care of a local couple until she was old enough for school. They were now looking for him to put him in reform school. Jack was outraged and wanted to go right then and steal her back.

"You can't do that" they told him. "You have to find your brother first and make a family for her. In the meantime she is being well taken care of by the couple that took her in. There are probably two or three dozen of these evangelist groups roaming around the country and until you find the one you want you can stay with us but you'll have to earn your way. Tilley used to be a teacher so with her to tutor you we can keep you out of reform school. If you were an alligator wrestler! We could get your story in the newspapers they would be glad to help you find your brother. The search would sell a lot of papers and possibly someone who knew something about it would come forward with information. The minister himself may even read about it and come forth. Of course they would only do it for a celebrity and we could make you in to one of those. We could put up a big banner just like Leo and Ti. You could become famous all over the world." All this talk was impressive to Jack but it in no way over shadowed his concern for Peggy Sue and his promise to come back and bring her book.

Back To Harborville

They had to cross the railroad tracks on the way to there new site. By using the watch like the old man showed him he knew the track ran east and west and the bus had taken him west to Springfalls. It stood to reason that if he rode the rails east he would get to Harborville or some where near it. He had seen how the guys looking for work had done it. As soon as it got dark Jack said he was going to sleep then picking up his little bundle containing Peggy Sue's book an apple and a bun then slid under the side of the tent and faded into the darkness. Once he got to the track he could see the lights of the station in the distance. There was a train sitting there so he knew it wouldn't be moving to fast by time it got to him. He hid in some bushes until the engine had gone by then made a dash for the first flat bed and threw his bundle on the deck and made a grab for the step. He got hold of the step but couldn't maintain his balance and was being dragged along beside the train. It went through his mind that if he just let go of the step he may fall under the wheels. With that in mind he hung on with his right hand and pushed himself away with his left as he let go of the step.

Now he was back on the ground and his bundle was on the train. The bundle he could replace but the book he had to have even if it cost his life. In an instant he was on his feet and running beside the train. The next car was full of cattle and he managed to get hold of a ladder at the end of it and pull himself up. Now he had only to get to the other end of the car. This meant putting his fingers between the boards and sidle the forty foot length of the car with only a one inch lip to walk on. The cattle nuzzled his hand as he went making his fingers wet and slippery as he moved along. Jack didn't know any thing about religion and God still he found himself talking to the cattle and the car and asking them to let him get to his bundle and see Peggy Sue again and give her the book like he had promised. Why he seemed to gain strength he had no idea but he didn't feel alone any more. When he had made the leap to the flat bed and laid his head on the precious bundle. He loudly thanked the cattle and the box car and the north-star! Then he thought of what Sickle used to sing out when he was feeling in the spirits and he shouted to the sky "Al he knew yah" it made no sense to Jack but it just felt so good. When he got to Harborville it was day light and he jumped off before they got to the station.

He began his search as discreetly as possible until he found Don and Hilda's house. There was no one home and a neighbor hollered at him not to leave anything as they had gone away for a holiday. Jack wrote a short note on a brochure that was lying on the step and stuffed it in the mail slot. It said "must find brother make famly. Jack" He took a peak in the shed and his cart was still there and just as he had left it. Next he looked for the lodge in hopes of finding someone there that would help him and may have news of Peggy Sue's father. When he found the lodge he stood behind a wire fence in case he had to run for it and waited for someone to come along. Eventually an elderly man came and unlocked the door.

Jack asked "Sir do you know Don and Hilda Walton? "

Yes I do he answered and I'll bet your Jack. You can come out from behind the fence he said I'm not going to turn you in. We'll see if we can scrape up some breakfast I'm starving. Once inside he turned on the stove and while Jack burned some toast he whipped up some bacon and eggs. Then while he introduced Jack to coffee with cream and sugar he told him of a man in the hospital. He was badly, burned and kept slipping in and out of a coma. But in his delirium he had said over and over she'll be safe with Jack. So Jack we have decided to help you make that the truth. But you must forever make that our secret. Then Jack told him of the offer he had been made at the Magic Max Circus.

We'll keep tabs on you and the man in the hospital and of course Peggy Sue.

Tell her I still have her book but I want to give it to her myself. Jack said

My name is Charlie Todd the man said and in most of the towns you go to there is a chapter of our lodge and if you go there and mention my name they will pass on any information we have.

Charlie got Jack a ride with a truck driver who was going to Elloree to deliver a load of market garden products. It was a lot nicer then riding the rails and he had someone to talk to. The truck driver appreciated a little conversation himself and when Jack asked him what all that stuff in the back was he rhymed of a couple of dozen things Jack had never seen or heard of. The only things he knew were carrots cabbage onions and apples. They were things Sickle used to bring from his mothers garden the odd time.

I love onions he told the driver but we only got a couple. The old man and I used to find leeks in the woods and fry them with our fish but they weren't as good as onions. When the driver stopped to let Jack out he reached in the back and gave Jack a bag with a half dozen Spanish onions in it.

"Try these" he said to him "they'll fend off the cold and keep you going for a while".

"What's your name" Jack ask?

"Just call me the Onion man" he said and then he was gone.

A New Star

When he got back to the Circus they were glad to see him and anxious to get started on his show. They gathered all the members of the company under the big top first thing in the morning before the crowds started showing up. While they were discussing and allotting jobs Jack ate two of his onions as if they were apples. When they got to discussing Jacks banner it was quickly decide they should depict Jack standing with his foot on the alligator's neck and wearing alligator pants and hat. That along with his enormous jack boots should tell the story. All that was left was to give him a name that would stick in people's minds. Leo who was in awe of the way Jack gobbled down those onions suggested maybe we should call him Onion Jack. People are bound to wonder why. We could depict him holding a big onion with a bite out of it.

Max cut in at this point. "What we'll do is write a story of how Jack gets his strength and courage from eating these onions and sell them at the show. First thing in the morning Tilley will get a banner made. Ti and Barney will rope of an area near the river so we can pump water to the pond. I have a horse drawn scoop coming to dig us a pool. To fill with water let's say about the same size as the one where you saved your sister. Of course we will have to make some safety precautions for Jack. We can't afford to loose him before we catch up to his brother. If we build this thing right we may not have to fill it back in when we leave. They could use it as an amphitheater or the like and it would be there when we come back in the future."

In some of the towns they played, the town would build the pond for them and that created a competition to see who could make the nicest one. Tilley proved to be a gifted teacher and she accredited it to Jack's eagerness to learn and the fact that he accepted her as she was and was not distracted by her appearance. Teaching in a school had been difficult for her due to the pupil's distraction and humor at her five o'clock shadow. Now they would have to pay for that privilege. In Jacks mind though, every one was an oddity in some way and he felt no need to remark on hers.

Jacks fame spread fast particularly after he became the catcher in the trapeze show. Then with the help of his friend Leo they built a tree house on top of a pole to depict a jungle scene .That done they strung wires to another pole that depicted a tree. They choreographed a show over the pond with Jack and a trained chimpanzee doing a swinging ballet with Ali in the water and no safety net. Unknown to the audience Ali was tether on a leash with a quick release pin on it. A security guard dressed as a golfer or a gardener would stand at the end of the pool with a shot gun. His presence assured the crowd of the danger. He also pulled the pin at a signal from Jack that released a stuffed animal from hiding and Ali unknowingly towed it a crossed the shore at the same time as he made his lunge. When Ali passed under the wires Jack would drop straddling him and the match would begin.

As their reputation grew they began to receive requests to celebrity parties to give private shows. These provided an opportunity make connections and inquiries about the evangelist's movements.

Europe

In spite of all the attention and fame Jack's determination to find his brother never waned and Peggy Sue's book was never far from his hand or his heart. He made contact with every lodge he could find and followed every tip he received. It was at one of these parties that Max got into a discussion with the host who claimed that his show would go over big in Europe and that he could line up many such parties as they were at. When Max explained to him their quest for an Evangelist minister with a son Jacks age he said he might be able to help and would get back to him. Two days later Max got a call and was told that an Evangelist was all ready in Europe. He had gone thereto avoid Social Services.

With in three weeks Max had a booking and they were on their way to France. Once they had set sail they made a pact to only speak French amongst themselves for the duration of the trip. This little trick help them to ignore the motion of the ship and created many a laugh even while describing your dinner menu as you spewed it over the rail. They would have three days to explore the country and acquaint them selves with the people. In three days they had convinced them selves they were going to like it in France. They were all at the docks when the freighter pulled in and Leo was waving to them from the deck. His had been a working trip but there were no regrets on his part since he seemed to prefer animals to people. The cute little red head that appeared at the rail beside him may have been the exception. It turns out he had gotten her on as an assistant. He felt she would be a good addition to the show since she was good with animals, great to look at and she spoke French. He introduced her as Rhonda La Blanc. Due to the animals in his caravan it had been arranged for him to be first off the ship and he was ready every thing was in order so that once they started moving there was no need to stop. The wagon designed for the gator wasn't as high as the others but it had a compartment on the bottom for accessories and a cage for a ten-foot long boa constrictor. There were drop down curtains on the side with pictures of Jack holding the boa over his head while resting his foot on the gators neck. They didn't wait until every thing was off the ship but headed for their first engagement Ti of course leading the way. For the last five miles he marched in front of the procession looking magnificent with his enormous handle bar mustache and toy soldier uniform, throwing his big baton in the air and catching it behind his back. Meanwhile the calliope enticed the people into the streets to watch them. The trapeze artists displayed their fantastic bodies with contortions cart wheels and walking on their hands. Jack sat on the roof of the alligator cage in his alligator pants and hat and waved to the crowd while he chomped on a huge onion and flexed his muscles. The clowns teased the kids and passed out balloons.

Max had to stay back to make sure nothing was left behind and settle with the captain. Their first stop was a concession park with in walking distance of four small villages each one as neat and friendly as the last and all anxious to set up their concession booths and peddle their wares. Each town had a specialty in order to mediate the competition. To their surprise and pleasure a pit had been dug and water made ready in the form of a fire hydrant. A hose was run to an artificial falls at one end of the pit. It seems the council had looked at the photo Max had sent and were not to be out done. There were all ready a couple of minstrels strumming and singing on the platform. There were six tiers of bleacher that could be moved back or forth depending on whether the show was in the pit or on the stage.

By nightfall the tent had been erected and the equipment moved into its allotted places. Some kids had been hired to distribute posters around the towns. Rhonda and Leo were nowhere to be seen so it was assumed they were washing and grooming the animals. Circus people are very gullible as a matter of diplomacy. After helping to raise the tent and taking care of Ali the Gator. Jack was free to pursue his obsession of finding his brother and establishing a family to adopt Peggy Sue.

France was a wonderful place to be with a circus. The people loved entertainment and were always anxious to join in. But it would seem all good things must come to an end and the German invasion of Austria drew a shadow over Europe that would spread around the globe.

When Germany attacked Poland Max decided it was time to go homo while they still could. The only things left behind was Ali the gator and his cage which were of no use without Jack. Rhonda opted to stay also and help Jack in his quest for his brother. Her aptitude for languages had been a boon to them during their travels. They also left the station wagon which could be replaced cheaper than shipped. Jack located a run down zoo that would keep the gator for him as long as he fed it in hope it may attract some more patrons. They had an abandoned pond that had once housed a hippopotamus and had now grown over with water plants and was actually quite pretty. Ali wasted no time in making himself at home. France was a different place for Jack with out his circus friends and a conversation with most anyone made his search for the Evangelist Minister an exercise in frustration.

Rhonda spent most of her time with her fiends and was often seen in the cafes in Paris. She had taken a job there serving beer and wine at the tables. She seemed to cater to the Germans and because she was an American and to their knowledge spoke only English and French. They spoke freely in her company. As a rule when a new waitress joined them they often tested her with derogatory remarks or compliments. When they felt daring enough to cop a feel she was quick and always careful to scold them only in a mixture of French and English. She had never told Jack she had joined the resistance but it was not necessary and her connections got him a few shows with the Nazis that had commandeered mansions for their headquarters. Jack felt no remorse about doing shows for the Germans since at times he had over heard information that was of use to the resistance. Jack and Rhonda worked out a strategy were they would remember the pronunciation of word they didn't under stand so it could be told to an interpreter along with what they did comprehend. They had also worked out a plan were by if a corner of paper that looked as if a notice had been ripped off was on the bulletin board near her work. That meant they should meet and Jack would sit down for a coffee. He always flirted with her and she would always politely turn him down. But he would try again next time there was a torn corner on the board.

Jack was on his way to check the bulletin board and his post box when he saw a brown shirt standing over a woman lying on the ground while another woman was holding a baby. The brown shirt was so intent on what he was doing that he hadn't noticed Jack stop the station wagon and get out. Jack came up behind the man and kicked him in the back of the knee. The man dropped to the ground and another kick to the throat left him choking and gasping for air. Then Jack turned to the girl holding the baby. She was young pretty, blonde and terrified.

Put her in the wagon she said to Jack nodding at the woman on the ground. His only reaction to that order was a dumb founded stare.

Do it now she said kicking him in the shins to get his attention. Jack shook his head and picked up the woman. She was bleeding badly and her nose appeared to be broken. He put her in the passenger side and the girl got in the back with the baby. Hurry she said there will be a dozen of them here in a minute. Turn right she told him then right again then stop. The instant he did the injured woman jumped out with the baby and ran in a doorway. Go the girl told him and turn left and don't stop but slow down. When he did she leaped out of the car hollering go and disappeared up a narrow alley. Two blocks down the road in his rearview mirror he could see a group forming at the last corner.

Above all else Jack wanted to see that girl again no matter what the cost to life or limb. He may have been able to put her out of his mind if hadn't been for the kick in the shins. As a result every free moment of his day was spent roaming the streets in that area in hope of catching a glimpse of her. He carried Peggy Sue's book with him during his search in hope an encounter would prove more than a mere fantasy. His fear of exposing her to the brown shirts kept him from asking too many questions. The shop in front of which he had first seen her was gutted and the house that the woman had run into was vacant. There was only one person left in France that Jack could speak to in a personal manner and his frustrations were getting out of hand. He felt he had to find the girl and know for sure one way or the other before he drove himself crazy. It was in this frame of mind that he confided in Rhonda. She listened intently and told him if she found anything worth investigating the paper would be on the board. Two days later it was there and he sat down for his cup of coffee. When she served him she was quick to inform him of a school for gifted girl two miles from the location he had mentioned and the girls often went there to shop. She also mentioned a brown shirt from that area, who had been promoted to SS and should be avoided at all cost. Also that it may be wise to avoid her from then on. Jack was quick to drink his coffee then left without looking back. When Jack located the school he waited outside in hope she would come out and he could confront her without making a fool of himself. Eventually he was confronted by an athletic looking woman in her forties who demanded to know if he was one of those brown shirts and what he was hanging around the school for. Jack told her as much as his French would allow. I have heard of you she said in English. You come to the side entrance after dark and I will bring her to meet you. She has wanted to thank you any way. After dark Jack parked the wagon two blocks from the school and walked to the side entrance where the girl and the teacher were waiting. In his hand he was carrying the book which he raised for her to see. The instant she saw the book she hollered "Jack" and threw herself into his arms. "You're Jack" she said "My Jack!"

Jack had never considered himself as belonging to anyone but himself. When she stepped back and kicked him in the shins and demanded "why did you take so long to find me?" He knew it was true and had been since she first kicked him in the shins and climbed into his wagon. All those many lonely year's ago.

"You've got to stop that" he said, fighting the temptation to crush her little body to him. Then the teacher cut in.

"We must go" she said "in these times you never know who may be watching. Go fishing by the river tomorrow after supper. If it's possible she'll meet you there."

She was there the next evening and she told him how the Lodge had paid her way to France to avoid the Social Service. They considered her a gifted person due to her love of ballet and her adeptness at the dance. He told her of his search for his brother and his desire to create a family for them all. They met again the following evening and sat on a rise above a gypsy camp listening to the music and watching them dance. They were sitting close together not speaking but just enjoying each others presence. A woman came up the hill directly toward them. When she stopped in front of them Jack asked "How did you know we were here?"

"When you're together your aura is so strong I could see it from the river she answered." Then she said to Jack "you know me don't you."

"Yes" he said. "But this time the beauty is also on the outside. Satan must be broken hearted. I always felt different near you and now I realize, your sole was gone. Possibly looking for this place while your mind and body stayed to finish what ever it was you had started." Then she turned to Peggy Sue who was sitting with one leg under her and the other stretched out.

"Get your foot in" she said "it is outside your aura."

"Do as she says Jack said harshly." She did as she was told but Jack had never used that tone of voice to her before and her feelings were hurt.

"She only wants some money" she said taking a dingy coin out of her pocket and handing it to the woman. The woman looked at it for a second then handed it back but now it was as shiny as new.

"I don't want your money" she said "but you must keep it with you at all times." When the woman was gone Peggy Sue asked "how did she do that and how do you know her."

"It is a long story" said Jack "and I'll tell it to you when it's finished. Right now we have to get you back. Else they'll put a curfew on you." It was strange to hear Jack talk this way but she knew it was her welfare on his mind. For the rest of the week she didn't show but Jack received a demand from the Gestapo to put on a show at the first town the circus had played when they arrived in France.

The Show

Jack and Ali appeared on the premises the day prior to the demand in order to be sure all was ready and safe for the next day. The town had prepared for the event. Their vender stands were out, the pond had been filled with water and lilies and a railing had been put across the front of the stage. Tables had been set on both sides of the stage and the back drop depicted a lake with green curtains on the sides masquerading as a forest while covering the entrance and exit for the cast. Ali was released into the pond as soon as Jack had checked the fences and the escape stile. Because, when you're running from a hungry alligator you don't want to worry about opening a gate.

When the staff car pulled up and the Nazis had taken their seats by the rail near the stage. The introduction to Swan Lake came on over the loud speakers. The SS officer was often referred to as the beast and his presence in the area caused much nervous loathing. Jack realized right away that he was the same brown shirt that had beaten the woman with the baby. In spite of the fact that it was a bright warm day. Jack suddenly felt cold and was glad that Peggy Sue would not be there. His truck load of soldiers did nothing to ease the tension either. They were the only ones allowed to approach him or serve him. Once the wine was served the show started. To Jacks surprise and horror Peggy Sue was starred as Odette and received much applause. Once the first act was over the beast called her to stand beside him at the rail while he praised their performance. That was when she realized, she didn't have her coin with her and she was afraid for the first time since she got it. In that same instant Jack realize that his security guard was gone.

Then the Beast turned facing the pond and said "you know Jack I think that in every drama the heroine should die at the end." Saying that" he picked Peggy Sue up and threw her in the pond. Peggy Sue, Ali and Jack all hit the water at the same time. Jack landed on the alligator and rained blows on his head and eyes. The gator was dazed but he had Peggy Sues leg in his jaws and kept thrashing until it came off about six inches below the knee. Alligators don't have molars to chew with so they bite through their prey and tear off a piece to swallow. While the gator was swallowing the leg Jack grabbed Peggy Sue and carried her over the stile. A doctor was already beating his way through the crowd.

The Beast was hollering "I'd shoot you now Jack but I want you to enjoy Peggy Sue's misery." That said he got back in his car and was driven away. In his rage Jack grabbed a broad axe from a venders display and leaped back over the stile. The gator seeing him come headed for the pond

Jack took one swing at him and removed the last two and a half feet of his tail. Then he broke down and wept. His grief was like nothing he had ever felt or could imagine.

Peggy Sue was in a coma when they took her to the local hospital. It was small but clean and the staff were sympathetic to Peggy Sues plight All decent people loathed the Beast but none as much as Jack and he swore a punishment equal to the deed. Peggy Sue was still in a coma a week later when Rhonda paid her a visit. She was feeling guilt for her part in her friend's misery. She felt that Peggy Sue remained in the coma to avoid the realization that she would never dance again.

A local butcher and taxidermist had taken the piece of Ali's tail that Jack had cut off and made a hat and a pair of pants of it which he presented to Jack along with a piece of the meat. Jack had no desire to look at them at the time but tasted the meat to appease the butcher. At a later date it occurred to him that in some way he might have felt it was only justice. He had to agree it tasted much like chicken but with a slightly courser grain. When the butcher left he stashed the hat and pants away out of his sight. The future would decide their mental and physical value to him and Peggy Sue.

Rhonda and Jack spent long hours discussing how they could best make the Beast atone for his sins. Rhonda had envisioned something in the line of a political failure on the beast's part that he would have to answer to Hitler for. Jack on the other hand figured that only his death could atone for his existence and purge the world of his presence. And so he schemed to lure the Beast to the zoo that for the exception of Ali had been abandoned. From there lure him to the old silo that had stored grain for the animals. Thanks to Max, Jack now knew the perfect man to accomplish such a maneuver and who had the best reason in the world to bring it about.

The Sting

A sting can't work without the presence of greed and in the composition of Rudolph Schultz "alias the Beast" there was only greed hate vanity and cruelty. He was totally lacking of any redeeming virtue at all and as such was the perfect candidate for a sting. The bait would have to be something tangible such as gold or jewels or a Swiss bank account. We intended to dangle all these things under his pig like nostrils.

The medium for our sting would be a wealthy Jew named Cecil and former curator of the zoo where Ali the now shorter alligator was being kept. Jack had grudgingly forgiven him due to Rhonda's plea that he was only being an alligator and acting his role in Jacks spectacle of strength and daring. Cecil who was being held under house arrest would be informed, through the web of the resistance that he would be sentenced to death and should plead for his life with a promise of gold and jewels and the key to a strong box. He should tell the Beast where to find the key to the silo and that the key to the strong box was on a nail to the left hand side of the door. That should cause him to reach in with his right hand moving it away from his gun. The moment his hand came in the opening the boa constrictor would have it. Jack had put a strong box in the silo and weighted it down with lead then he put a good strong lock on it and covered it with grain leaving a small corner exposed. Next he put in the boa constrictor that had grown to about sixteen feet in the last few years and hadn't been fed in a couple of months. Boas have fangs at the back of their mouths that angle inward and dig in if their prey tries to escape then they wrap themselves around it and suffocate it. This was the fate that Jack had created for the beast. But it would give him no satisfaction.

Cecil was a master at negotiation and a greedy man had two strikes against him before he started. Cecil not only gained his own freedom but got to see his family fly away on a private plane with his son at the controls. He then accompanied the Beast to the zoo with one guard. When the guard had made sure there was no one around Cecil accompanied him to the silo and was then taken back to the car. The Beast entered the room alone wearing only shirt and pants. His coat had been left behind lest it attract too much attention. They knew he would for fear someone may steal from him. Jack heard him open the two foot square silo door there was one terrified scream then silence. He closed the door and locked it. Then hung a sign on it saying beware of snake and left. After the scream the guard went in he took one look at the locked door and the sign and returned to the car. He called Jack out telling him he was with the Resistance then got behind the wheel. Cecil was already dressed in the beasts coat and hat.

"We'll drop the car at the train station" he said "they will pick us up from there. To Cecil he said "they will have some cloths and papers for you. You can take the train to Switzerland. Someone will meet you at the end of the line."

"I don't know how you came to be involved Jack said but I'm glad you did. What will you do now" Jack asked?

"I only know I've lost the job that the Resistance worked so hard to get me, but if I go back they'll hang me in Cecil's place. At any rate as an interpreter I'll never run out of work in these times."

With that he drove off leaving Jack to his own devices.

The Awakening

Jacks life now was spent mostly at the side of Peggy Sue's bed in hope of being there when she woke. He spoke to her constantly and at times her twitching and eye movements led him to believe that wherever her mind had taken her she was dancing. He also felt that if he couldn't waken her the dance would never end until she died.

Cecil out of gratitude and respect had taken all Jacks debts upon him self and had contacted the curator of another zoo who with the resistance had moved the snake and removed all signs of the beasts presence at the silo. Along with all that, he had taken up the search for Jack's Evangelist Minister and son.

Jacks days were spent sitting and talking to Peggy Sue or getting an onion from a vendor and going for a stroll. At first he used to chat with the locals but now he would just wandered off by himself. The tension was taking its toll on his nerves and health. After one such stroll he stood looking down at her. And while the tears rolled down his cheeks. He hollered at her.

" For Gods sake woman where is the fight. If it had been me the girl I love would have kicked me in the shins by now and hollered giddy up. Well the shoe is on the other foot now so giddy up." When he wiped his eyes and went to turn away he realized she was looking at him.

"Did You Yell At Me?" She said.

"You bet I did" he croaked while laughing and crying and hugging her.

"I can't dance Jack" she said. "When I try I keep falling over and I loved being Odette."

"You'll always be my Odette" he said.

"And you'll be my prince as always. But what did you do to our dragon?" She wanted to know.

"He's a little shorter" Jack said "But he'll survive. It has been this way since I first laid eyes on you and received a kick in the shins to check my emotions. In spite of all that has happened we can now make this our time." Then they talked about her leg and their options and about going back to America as soon as they found out what had happened to the Evangelist Minister and his brother. The next months were devoted to building up their strength and fallowing up leads to his brothers where abouts and just enjoying each other. For Jack the absence of her leg had its good side. He often had to carry her in his arms something they always enjoyed since it created some very tender or comical moments for them both. An envelope had mysteriously appeared at Peggy Sues flat, addressed to her and when she opened it. It contained the shiny coin and a note that said I'm so very sorry I took it. Please forgive me.

Jack said "I wonder who took it."

But Peggy Sue said "it doesn't mater any more. I have it put on a chain to wear around my neck. Psychology or magic if it works and raises your confidence the means is of no consequence."

With Cecil as his backer Jack had gained French citizen ship and joined the Free French Army in nineteen forty four. This not only allowed him an opportunity to help the people he so much admired but to establish his existence. Since there was no record of his birth any where on earth. The war ended a year later and Jack received an honorable discharge and a citation. In the mean time Peggy Sue worked for the school she had to leave as a pupil and through correspondence kept up the search for Jacks brother.

A New Beginning

By the time the grapes were ripe and ready to be crushed. Jack and Peggy Sue were ready to meet the world and how better than to crush a few grapes. Taste some stinky foot wine and laugh a lot.

One footed women don't crush a lot of grapes but they create a lot of laughter and require a little bit of assistance and a workable plan. The plan appeared infallible until it was put into action. Peggy Sue would simply sit on the edge of the tub with the short leg on the outside and crush the grapes with the good leg. Unfortunately when she pressed with the good leg it didn't go down but pushed her out of the tub. Not to worry! Jack with glass in hand would simply lean against her while she did her half share of stomping. The plan was working But Jacks glass just would not empty and the harder he tried to empty it the harder he leaned on Peggy Sue. Until finally they both ended up in the tub and almost drown since Jack was lying on Peggy Sue and couldn't get up. The women all grabbed Jack and threw him face down in the tub while they fussed over Peggy Sue. Every time Jack got his head out of the juice some woman would chastise him for not taking proper care of Peggy Sue and push him back in the juice. Finally a couple of guys grabbed and laid him over the edge of the tub to drain.

By the time Jack had drained enough to think of going home the sun had turned the dark into a pale pink glow. It gave just enough light to make out the wine soaked bodies lying every where in every contortion imaginable and emitting sounds that could shatter a sober head or explode a hung over one. The walk home for two people with three legs and a crutch was ordinarily a half hour saunter. But on this morning it was a two hour stagger. It must have been the sun in their eyes. They took no time to admire their pale purple bodies but simply slept where they dropped. To wake up in dried wine soaked cloths is an experience in misery that can only be forgotten by the next wine stomping party. At which time they swear to reestablish and maintain their dignity. Amen

There were other grape crushing parties but for the sake of their dignity they avoided the grape tub and danced instead. Peggy Sue's stump was to tender yet for an artificial leg. Jack though couldn't deprive her of the pleasure she got from dancing. So they choreographed a dance of their own were she would put her crutch on his toe and he would do that step for her. With Peggy Sue's natural grace and coordination the crutch became almost invisible and where ever they went, they attracted admirers.

Family Affairs

Jack and Peggy Sue had never tied the knot because Jack wanted to marry her under his family name. Since the Peach had died with out leaving so much as a picture her name or where she had come from. Jack figured it should be the same as his brother and so they waited. They both realized that the minister may not want to give Jack his name. But due to the fact that Jacks brother was not of his blood they felt he would have no objection to having twin sons. This was a factor that would have to be dealt with when they found him since it would be a terrible shock to the mother to find out that the son she had raised was the fruit of another woman's womb and not even the seed of her husband. It wasn't long before things began to happen.

The Lodge had been notified that the burn victim in the hospital had come out of his coma and asked for some one named Peggy Sue. Two Lodge members visited him right away and wrote his will for him. Which he signed Hector Craig! They told him all they could about Peggy Sue. When they told him about Jack and how he saved her from the gator. What passed as a smile came over his burn scared face and through pursed lips he said only God could keep her safer than Jack. Peggy Sue received a telegram from the lodge informing her of his death and that he had been cremated. Also that the property was hers and they had paid the taxes to date. Along with that was the key to a strong box in the local bank.

While Peggy Sue was hashing over her options and responsibility as to her father's death Jack received a call from Cecil informing him that the Minister he had been looking for was now in New York State with his son. If Jack felt he must talk to him he should make it soon as his health was fading. This piece of information settled all the maters of concern.

They caught a flight to Savannah the next day. There they rented a car and headed to Harborville to visit Hilda and Don. They would make a brief stop along the way at a town called Blessing. After they had met the gypsy woman Jack had ordered a bronze plaque made to commemorate the Crone. She was buried in an unmarked grave but they would have no trouble finding it. Since it was the only place in the cemetery were flowers grew. Jack took the plaque with him because he felt such a good person deserved recognition it read.

Jessica Wade

An angel rests here

The town's people aware of the miracle that gave them their homes eventually incorporated the plaque into a statue of an angel and often laid flowers and trinkets on her grave. The fact that the town was called Blessing seemed appropriate to Jack.

A visit would allow them to get more information and renew some old acquaintances. Don contacted the Lodge brothers who had visited Peggy Sue's father and arranged to meet them at the Lodge. Peggy Sue needed to know what was in the strong box before she made any long-range plans. She and Don met them for lunch two days later. They presented her with her father's ashes and accompanied her to the bank in the event she required witnesses, or just moral support. Her father had left a will leaving all he owned to her. Her inheritance included a diagram of what she had no idea and a model A Ford coupe that had been covered with a tarp all these years. With a little bit of know how from her new friends it ran like a top. Fortunately Jack had made her a peg leg and with a ridge welded around the pedal to keep it from sliding off she could work the clutch. With a change of ownership a license plate and Hilda as navigator she was about to see a lot of America on that twenty mile trip home. Peggy Sue was anxious to get back to Hilda's in hope there was news from Jack. But in a couple of hours her anxiety had changed to frustration then to resignation. At about three A.M. they would make a tearful call to Don to come to Peekskill and show them the way home. He informed them he had already called all the hospitals and police, but would start out as soon as he told Hilda's brother why they phoned. He would be glad to know they were still in Virginia.

Meanwhile Jack was having a snooze in the car in order to save time. He was on his way to a town called Millwood and would call when he got there. When Jack arrived in Millwood it was coming on evening and he assumed the service would be in progress. The tent was still standing, so he knew they hadn't moved to another site. A coffee and a sandwich gave Jack an opportunity to ask some questions. He was informed that the minister was in Briar Hill hospital and the son had gone to visit him.

Jack took a coffee for the road and headed for the hospital. His mind was full of confusion it seemed that every thought he came up with his mind would contradict. Pros and cons had no basis in his head. How do you tell a dying man that his past has caught up to him or a minister that confession is good for the soul? His mind only became more confused as he approached the glass doors of the hospital and felt he was approaching his reflection in the door. His mind was still playing tricks on him for when the door swung out of the way he was facing himself in the flesh. Every thing was identical right down to the startled look on his face. When the two men facing each other had recovered from their initial shock, the man on the inside stepped back and Jack followed him.

"How is your father" Jack asked?

"He's resting" came the reply. Then they both turned to compare their reflections in the glass. Even their cloths were almost identical.

"Who the hell are you the man asked?"

"I don't really know" Jack said "I was hoping your father could tell me."

"Sit down and explain this to me" the man said.

"I can't until I speak to your father I'm hoping then I'll know what I'm talking about."

With that said Jack followed himself or so it seemed to a room where a white haired old man was lying in a bed with tubes up his nose and in his arms.

"How do you feel dad" the young man asked?

"All right" the old man said "but I seem to be seeing double.

"Your eye sight is all right" Jack said. "I need to talk to you in private."

"What about" the old man asked? With that Jack showed him the note the old crone had left.

"Should I leave" the young man ask?

"No" the old man said "what you should do is call my lawyer." Then with a tear in his eye he said "I had no idea there were two of you and you come so late."

"I have been searching for you since I saw the note, even so far as to France" said Jack.

"The old crone had asked me to come over as she was sure the Peach was going to die and she had been the mid wife for my wife that same day and my boy had died. He was buried in the same plot as his Grand Mother." "There is no record of my birth," Jack told him "nor any knowledge of my mother's name or birth place. As a result I had hoped to find my brother and possibly share his name. Since I intend to get married I wish to give my wife a name with some basis to it."

"And so it will be" said the minister switching his gaze from Jack to his son. "I guess now you know why your mother always scrutinized you so closely. She was looking for some family resemblance. In your later years you picked up some of our habits and that satisfied her. She always took pride in calling you son. I feel some how that God thinks I should set the record straight before he passes judgment on me."

"I need a little rest before the lawyer gets here" he said. "You boys have a coffee and get acquainted. Lord knows you couldn't be more closely related."

Over coffee Jack learned that the minister's name was Richard Blessing and his brother was Derrick. But the people who know me insist on calling me reverend. Jack tried the name the way girls do when they meet a guy that they might consider marrying. Jack Blessing! That was questionable but Peggy Sue Blessing Seemed an appropriate name for her. When the lawyer showed up with his secretary they wrote up papers declaring an oversight in the registering of the birth. Next he held a christening in the hospital room. Then turning to Jack he said "I will send you a birth certificate as soon as possible Mr. Jack Blessing."

The Rescue

It took Don about an hour to get to the restaurant where the girls were waiting. When he entered they were sitting at a table with a drunk that was telling them of when he used to operate a Zamboni and the day it got away from him and almost destroyed the store he was working in. Every time he attempted to get up and demonstrate, he would fall on the floor and they would have to pick him up and put him back in the chair. Don's rescue interrupted the finale but the teller of tales had fallen asleep anyway. Don led the women home alone in his car because Hilda had no desire to explain how they had gotten lost. When they arrived home the sun was rising and Kelly was there waiting for any news from Jack.

The call came about ten in the morning and Jack was all excited. He wanted her to come as fast as possible they could be married by his father and brother in the hospital.

Then he said "Stop in New York City and get a dress."

She said "I've got a dress Jack. I bought it six weeks ago if you remember?"

Jack asked "What color was it, do you need shoes?"

"Green Jack." she replied "and one shoe will do."

"Where do you get green roses?" he asked.

"In Ireland Jack." she responded.

"I don't have time." Jack remarked.

Someone is pulling your leg." Peggy Sue said.

"I hope it's not an alligator." Jack responded soberly.

"That's not funny Jack" she pouted.

"I know, I love you and I'm going to hang up now." he said.

The phone rings again two minutes later. "It's Jack. I forgot to tell you where I'll be." he said.

"Don, Hilda and Kelly want to come too. If that is okay you should give the directions to Don." Peggy Sue responded.

The Minister was determined to hang on long enough to meet his daughter in law. Then he said he would be here to pronounce them husband and wife providing they would let him sleep now.

It was two days later when Jack whispered in his ear they are here. His eyes were slow to open but the light in them was still shining brightly. When he laid eyes on Peggy Sue they seemed to throw sparks. He took her hand and said "I know Grace will forgive me now." With that he lay back still holding her hand and watched his son Derrick perform the ceremony. At the end he motioned Jack over and putting Peggy Sue's hand in his said "I now pronounce you man and wife. Now we may kiss the bride" and they did. Then he thanked the congregation that had now been joined by half of the hospital staff and any patients that could make it.

With his last breath he said- "Live with love it will make it right for all, even for me with Grace."

I'm going to see her soon and she has probably been busy convincing the Lord that my sins have all been made with the best of intentions.

The congregation gave that a big "Amen".

Then with a smile on his lips he went to meet his maker.

The Reception

Don had informed the Lodge of Peggy Sue and Jack's return and intentions. As a result they had arranged a reception at the local lodge. They had invited everyone who had known Jack and Peggy Sue who had been their special protégée. They had even found Sickle, his mother and the old man. They were now living in The Big Apple and Sickle was dancing on Broudway. "The street that is"

They also found the circus in the act of folding their tent and invited them. When they appeared it was as a parade with Ti and his great baton leading a great calliope drawn by four huge horses and playing Hail, Hail the gangs all here. They stopped in front of the hospital then carried Jack and Peggy Sue out and set them on top of the calliope. They were paraded all the way to the Lodge. At the lodge Peggy Sue and Jack gave them a demonstration of their three legged choreography. .It wasn't long before every one had to give it a try. Few showed an aptitude for it but they all had fun. When the party got into full swing the newly weds slipped away. Not entirely unnoticed since the racket made by the garbage tied to the back of the car alerted everyone. They were unmolested for the next two days but on the third day Jack received a notice to see the lawyer for the reading of the will and the funeral of Richard Blessing.

Richard had arranged to be cremated and have his ashes put in a niche in the wall of the cemetery where his wife was buried. According to the will Jack was given a house and pond on a hundred acres of property. This came to him with the blessing of Derrick as a wedding gift. After the reading of the will Derrick took him and Peggy Sue to see the property. It was in need of a little TLC but they could see its potential and Peggy Sue came up with a hundred suggestions every time she turned around. By the time they left it had gone from a one bedroom cottage to four bed rooms with a patio office, recreation room a swing in a tree a two car garage a manicured lawn and four kids playing in the yard. Jack hadn't given up his family dream or his brother. He had waited to long to stop now.

When the two of them got a few minutes a lone Peggy Sue showed him the diagram that was with the will in the bank vault. Jack mulled it over for a while then he said "I think it looks like the frame work of the car. I also think your dad meant this car to get away in if the revenuers got to close so there may be money stashed some where in it. Let's go and examine it." On close examination they found a panel in the rumble seat compartment that looked like a foot rest but didn't show on the diagram. Removal of the screw that held it in place exposed an oil skin bag that was full of money. For the time being they would leave it where it was.

A New Life

Before they left Jack had to talk to the circus people that had been his family for such a long time. There had been little time for conversation at the wedding and they were all close to his heart. They had settled into a vacant lot just outside of town and set up the small tent as a kitchen and meeting room. They would move on to their next appointment in a couple of days. Jack and Peggy Sue thanked them all profusely for the wonderful reception. While Jack sat down to talk with Max, Tilley, Ti and Leo, Peggy Sue acquainted herself with the rest of the crew. It took very little time for Jack to realize the circus was in trouble. Max told him they were not making enough to support the crew and those who could find work had left and the rest were working for meals. Between the war, the depression and the fact that they hadn't had a main attraction since he left. People just wouldn't spend what little money they had on the circus. Leo told him he was going back to France to try and find Rhonda. Life just wasn't the same without her. That statement turned a light on in Jacks head. If Leo could either send or bring Ali back they could store their equipment at his place for the winter and he would join the show in the spring. Of coarse he would have to talk it over with Peggy Sue before he committed himself. Peggy Sue went along with it. It was an opportunity to help their friend and since Jacks only experience so far had been with bootlegging and circus, neither of which was of much help in these times. The proposition offered some hope for the future. Kelly had stayed for awhile to help get the house in order it had been used as a hunting lodge for a long while and need the feminine touch to make it livable for real people as the women say. It was now time to return Kelly to her own home and job. They turned the rental in at the drop off and headed back to Harborville in Peggy Sue's coupe as she called it. When it rained they all piled in the front and when the sun shone they let the hood down and took turns in the rumble seat. It was dark when they pulled into Don and Hilda's and they were tired so the conversation was cut to a minimum. Since conversation was more enthusiastic at the breakfast table. After breakfast Jack and Don wandered out to the tool shed where they had stored the wagon it was covered in dust and cob webs. It seemed to chastise Jack for going on the adventure they had planned so long ago with out it. It reminded him that Woof wouldn't stay in the house but died beside it waiting to get back in the harness. It told him how Peggy Sue would come and sit on it and tell Woof the things she was doing and how Jack would soon come and bring her book back. Then they would go camping again. I'm here now Jack thought and so is Peggy Sue and the book. And when we have children we'll get another woof and you can go adventuring again. But you won't have to worry about Social Services or wars.

I'll put it in the rumble seat Jack said and I'd like to give you something for all you've done. "You've given Hilda the daughter she wanted and me bragging right at the lodge. I think that'll cover your bill with us. Besides I'll be up to do some hunting one of these days."

Reproduction

When Jack returned home the circus crowd had move every thing onto his property with the exception of the animals which they had boarded out to a zoo for the winter. They had set up the little tent as temporary quarters and Leo had gotten a job on a cargo ship to France. He needed only a blank check from Jack to cover Ali's expenses and he could leave the next day. He had supervised the fencing of the pond to keep Ali in and all others out. The crew was gradually fading away. Some got jobs others went to visit relatives. Max and Tilley hooked up the trailer and headed for Florida. Ti would join them later but for now he stayed to give Jack a hand with the heavy jobs.

Eventually Jack and Peggy Sue were left with nothing to do but reproduce. When they weren't busy on the production line they would make toys and cloths for little boys and girls. For some unknown reason Peggy Sue's eggs were just not hatching and the Doctors could find no biological reason for it. That left only psychological reasons which neither of them could understand. In the meantime Jack was spending more and more time at the pub while Peggy Sue sulked and watched their dreams deteriorate around them. Jack eventually built a still in the woods way back from the house where he and his buddies could make their own sipping whisky get drunk and tell lies about their adventures and women of course. Ali finally showed up but without Leo who still hadn't found Rhonda. Ali was no longer a circus star and for the exception of some road kill and the odd rabbit the boys shot to prove how tough they were his diet and welfare were ignored. The boa had died shortly after being moved to the new zoo .The vet diagnosed it as having eaten something that disagreed with it. Jack and Peggy Sue were no longer the beacons of society they had been but two disheveled lonely and grumpy people. When their depression had dropped about as far as it could go the Canadians showed up.

A Blessing in Disguise

Jack could hear them coming up the driveway and his first compunction was to ignore them. But on second thought he figured he might as well get some money from them and it might even break the boredom. In that frame of mind he grabbed an onion and went out to meet them. There were five of them all staring at him as if he were an apparition. It was an old car with an Ontario license plate. It looked as run down to Jack as he probably did to the occupants.

The first one out of the car approached him saying "you must be Onion Jack."

"The one and only" Jack replied stretching out his hand. "And you?"

"I'm Scotty. You look shorter than you do on your sign."

"We all shrink a little with time" Jack answered breathing in his face. This guy must be the diplomat of the group he thought, getting a little satisfaction from seeing his eyes water "and don't knock the sign it has seen more of the world than any of you."

"Where is your alligator hat and pants" Doug the next guy asked?

"The gator et them the same time he et the wife's leg" he said pointing at Peggy Sue sitting on a bench in front of the house. She gave a limp sort of wave and went back to reading her book on psychological black outs. From where they were standing they over looked the pond.

Vic wanted to know if he wrestled the gator in the water.

"Yep" Jack said "ever since we et his tail he's been a little shy about coming out of the water."

"You et his tail George" said sticking his head out the back window?

"Yep" Jack said "a tail for a leg is fair play. There is some thing in the Bible about that or so the reverend says. But he always seems so nervous when he comes around here that you're never sure what he means."

"Do you think he could out run a cow?"

"That's Gord" Dough said "he almost lost a race to a cow this morning. By the way I'm Doug."

"Out run a race horse in a short sprint" Jack said. "I have some friend coming at two to see the show." Then leaning into Vic window he said "I'll be a might offended if you fellows don't show up."

"We'll be here" we all said "jus got some shopping to do."

"Where you fellows headed any way" Jack said? "Florida" Vic said a little to hastily as he started down the drive way.

When they were gone Jack said to Peg as he called her now. I had best go to town and make sure those fellows can find their way back. When Jack got to town he found the old Desoto backed against the wall behind the grocery store supposedly out of sight. This suited Jack he simply parked cross ways in front of them and went to the pub to join the boys for a beer. In his arrogance Jack had left the keys in the ignition and the windows and doors unlocked assuming that no one would touch his truck. With two snakes and a spider nest in the cab the locals had learned to steer clear of it. The Canadians though just didn't understand to leave bad enough alone. When Jack came out of the pub his truck was butted up to a lamp post and it had a board sticking out of the window and two flat tires. They had obviously used the board to depress the clutch and pushed the truck out of their way. By the time he had hand pumped the tires up they would be well on their way to Florida. Jack was scheduled to give the Reverend a little assistance at the ceremonies in the tent this night and had to get prepared.

The Reverend had learned from his father that their most sacred duty was to maintain the church and get the message out to the people. If they had to bend the rules a bit in order to do that it was forgivable. Unknown to Jack the Canadians where in the congregation that night and when he came out on the stage disguised as a blind pauper he heard one of them say that's Jack.

That's when he lost it and dropping his disguise he grabbed a ceremonial snake out of the box and leaping off the stage took after the Canadians. At the same time as they ran out the door. The snake was about six feet long and Jack was holding it by the head and flailing it like a whip. When he lashed it around a post the snake hung on pulling its head through Jacks hand and driving its fangs into hi palm. Jack didn't slow down. He was obsessed with catching those guys and taking his revenge upon them. Finally they stopped running. When he caught up with them the run had worked the poison through his system. He just stared at them and collapsed jus as Peggy Sue pulled up in the truck.

It was an apparition that opened the truck door. Peggy Sue was sitting with her peg on the clutch pedal that had been raised around the edges to prevent it from slipping off. Her hair was hanging over her face and she was holding a snake in her left hand while trying to steer wit her elbow. With her right hand she was trying to shift gears with a snake wrapped around her wrist. "Throw him in the back" she said "he'll be alright it's the snake that's liable to die." The guys tried to put him in the back without touching the truck. But that only proved harder on Jack. Once Jack was in the back Peggy Sue headed for home.

When she got there she hadn't notice the gate to the pond was open and drove past it then stopped the car. That's when Jack fell out and went staggering through the gate. He fell down near the water and crawled over to wash his face. He was totally unaware of the yellow eye watching from just below the surface. Jack moved a little to slow this time and Ali had him by the belt and began thrashing him around like an old rag until he passed out. Peggy Sue had come to Jacks assistance but when she took a kick at Ali her peg leg sank in the mud and she fell on her back. She could only lay there and watch in horror as they both disappear beneath the surface.

When Peg finally calmed down after watching Jack get dragged under by the alligator and realized they weren't coming up again. She began scanning the property. That was when she found his belt buckle and the stud from his boots. She also realized that the sow they had made such a pet of had disappeared. She gave the matter little thought, since it wasn't the first time it had gotten out on them. What she failed to realize was that its cloven hoof prints had ended at the waters edge.

The only thing occupying her mind at the moment was a gnawing desire to get away from this place and put a little sanity into her life. Life with Jack had never been dull but it sure was trying. For now she would pack a few necessities, Jump in the truck and go. She didn't know where but it just didn't matter. Any place was better than here now that Jack was gone. She had never considered being without him before. Once back in the house she grabbed an old carpet bag and started packing. When she figured she had enough to get by on. She grabbed a tobacco tin out of Jacks gun cabinet to put her trinkets in such as the buckle and stud and the alligator brooch he had given her as a wedding present. When she opened the can her heart got stuck in her throat and her legs couldn't support her anymore. She sank down into a big over stuffed chair and tried to calm the quivering that had taken over her body. When she finally caught her breath and gained control of herself she realized that Jack was still taking care of her and the tears made rivulets down her cheeks. These weren't the crocodile type, but warm salty tears the kind he kissed away when they first made love. She relaxed and her mind wandered back through the years with the man that even the sign on the highway could never do justice to. He had always been and still was her knight in shining armor. It had only been a few months earlier that Jack had put the wagon in the gator pen to get it out of his way. The next morning he found it all smashed to pieces and the money he had forgotten about scattered allover the pen. It would seem that Ali had taken his frustrations out on the wagon. That was when Jack had put it in the tobacco cans

The sun shining through the dust streaked window finally woke her and she realized she was sitting with a tobacco tin stuffed full of money in her lap and four more in the gun cabinet ye to be examined. The first thing she must do was freshen herself up. Then throw her carpet bag in the truck and head to town. The reverend needed to know what had happened. After all they were brothers and Jack deserved a memorial of some sort. When she arrived in town she found the reverend in the pub having a drink with Jacks old cronies. Once she had told them the story of Jacks demise the reverend raised his glass in a salute to Jack as they all did. Then he informed them that Jack always wanted a good old fashion wake at his parting. So they drank to that then they drank to the good times then to the bad times. By this time Peg was plastered.

"Give us one of your step dances," one of the boys said as he pulled out the piano stool. Another one pulled out a harmonica and another pair of spoons. She protested but they lifted her up on the table.

"Do it for Jack" they said and one of them got her wooden leg going to the beat and she was off like she always did for Jack. Then the reverent stood up.

"It ain't right we should have a wake for Jack with out him being here." He said

"We'll have to take it down to the pond."

"I ain't ever going there again" Peg said. "The property should go to the reverend and Jack would like for all of you to enjoy it like always." With that she picked up her bag and headed to the bus stop across the street. The long ride to the Big Apple would give her time to think and plan a future for her self. She was a few years Jacks junior and had lots of life left in her yet. With one of those prostitute legs or what ever they call them and a little beautifying she could step out with the best of them. She didn't know where Jack got the money but she had heard rumors of a still in the back woods during prohibition.

Meanwhile back at the pub the boys had thrown a keg of beer in the truck and headed for the pond in order to say goodbye to Jack and let the reverend administer his last rites.

The Resurrection

Now it's common knowledge among alligator enthusiasts that gators keep caves with the entrance jus under the surface and the floor sloping up almost to ground level. As a rule the only thing holding the sod up was the roots of the surrounding plant life. These caves served as a larder for crocodiles that had over indulged. This particular croc had just devoured a hundred pounds of prime pork and hadn't even had a good belch yet. He wanted to be at his best for lunching with Jack "Jack being the lunch of course and since he didn't have a tail to nourish digestion may take a little longer than usual. Good beef should be aged about fourteen day anyway. Providing you could wait that long. He'd had a taste of Peggy Sue and she was definitely dessert, but Jack was the main course. Just the thought of it made him salivate.

The little group of friends walked down to the edge of the pond and when the reverend bowed his head to pray, he noticed the cloven hoof prints in the sand. Stifling a sob he raised his head to the heavens as he had done many times before.

"Lord he wailed Satan has visited upon us this day and a mighty battle has been fought for Jacks body and soul. Whether he be hiding in Jack or the gator or both. He must be exorcized before Jack knocks on your pearly gates. I cannot accomplish this task alone Lord. I need your mighty hand to smite the demon."

"Hallelujah" roared the reverends congregation of three. Then there came a deafening clap of thunder and a mighty torrent of rain fell upon the little congregation.

"It's getting in the beer" said one of the boys "lets get in the house before it ruins the whole keg."

While the boys were celebrating on Jacks behalf the rain had washed away all the soil from the roof of the cave and wakened Jack from his stupor. The rain had also washed the dirt from Jacks face and cleared his eyes. When he opened his eyes he had no idea of where he was or if he was alive or dead. The only thing he could make out appeared to be a dark black spider web. Maybe I've died and come back as a spider he thought .I hate spiders they are the reason I keep the snakes in the truck to eat them. I'd have preferred to be a raccoon or even a skunk anything but a spider. That was when the clouds parted and the light of a full moon fell on Jack and he let out a great hallelujah like the swamp had never heard before. "I see the light he roared. I'm a coming Lord the reverend will speak for me."

Meanwhile the little congregation had come out and was standing heads bowed while the reverend prayed for the lord to drive the demon from this place and let Jack abide in the great swamp in the sky. In one fleeting moment a meteor pierced the cloud and stabbed into the pond, Jack leaped out of the hole in the ground and the congregation fell to its knees and swore off drinking. During the struggle to get Jack to his larder Ali had at first grabbed Jack by the belt tearing his buckle off. Then in the process of getting him across the pond had torn his shirt off. When Jack leaped out of the ground his pants fell down leaving him naked to the entire congregation. The reverend raise his arm to the sky and for the first time in his life all he could say was "surely Lord Jack couldn't be the rebirth of Christ could he." Upon viewing this phenomenon the little congregation fell to their knees and ask for forgiveness. When they raised their heads a tailless sickly white alligator crawled out of the pond and lay shivering on the bank.

They all gathered around Jack in awe to welcome him back to the land of the living.

"I've seen the light" Jack said to the reverend.

" I know" said the reverend "I exorcized you."

"Well I don't need any more exercise" said Jack. "What I need is a good stiff drink."

"Right on" said the little congregation as one voice. "We're with you."

And the party continued till they got to the bottom of the keg. Then Milton he was the educated one he got right up to grade five. Of course with tending the still and distributing the produce he didn't have a lot of time for classes. But he reckoned if you came to your own wake you shouldn't be drinking the booze. It was the congregation's duty to pour it on your grave, once they'd filtered it through their kidneys. Even though they had put the keg on Jacks tab it being his wake and all. He hadn't given them a proper place to leave the filtered beer. This bought them all back to the hole where Jack had reappeared and they all relieved them selves while the reverend said a little rebirth sermon for Jack.

"Lord" he said "we thank you for returning Jack to us. I know that he will be a better man for his ordeal."

The whole town noticed that Jack had changed since his ordeal. His memory was bad and he was nervous around alligators. He often mentioned a girl he used to know that walked funny and for some unknown reason every time he ran into a bright light he'd curse them damn Canadians. Most just assumed he was addled from his ordeal. But others sensed divinity in Jack and the reverend did nothing to change their minds. Jack still loved his onions and when he passed around the collection plate he bought tears to the eye of the congregation and improved the donations and that was divine. If they were still stingy he would just stand there and breath on them.

When Peg had been in The Big Apple for a while she ran into Sarah singing on Broadway for change from the pedestrians. They moved in together and Peg became her manager and landed a few gigs on stage. At one performance Sarah called up a new friend she introduced as the man with the magic feet Peggy Sue recognize him right away even after all these years as Sickle their friend and partner in crime and she became his manager also. It proved a good move for all, since they all made money.

Peg did return to the old house one more time to leave a memorial stone for Jack. When she seen that poor old alligator lying on the bank afraid to go in the water she had it delivered to her home. After all she did have a large backyard and a swimming pool and it was better than a watch dog. Besides people thought twice about arguing with a one legged agent, that kept half a sickly white alligator as a pet. She often claimed it made her feel like her family was all together in an alligator bag.

The Revelation

One afternoon Peggy Sue was feeling a little remorseful about the things that were missing in her life so she treated herself to a movie. She took a seat behind a husband and wife with two young children. While waiting for the show to start the children turned around and looked at her.

The little boy said " this is my mom ain't she beautiful."

Then the woman turned to her and said "you'll have to excuse my son I think he has a crush on me." Peggy Sue was shocked when she saw the woman's face it had been terribly distorted by some thing like fire or acid. But her blue eyes were so clear you could see all the way to heaven in them. Suddenly all the remorse left her and she realized why she had no children.

She said "thank you so much" to the woman. "You will never realize how beautiful you are." Then taking the kids faces in her hands he said "and you are beautiful too." Then got up and left. This incident had made her realize that she was afraid her children wouldn't love her with just one leg. Now she realized love isn't measured by what you're missing but by what you have and share. I have to talk to the reverend about this she thought while heading home to pack a bag. She had avoided him last time she was there because he bought back such sad memories and she was envious of his wife and children.

It was evening when she got there and the meeting had been going on for a while in fact they were taking around the collection plate. She had taken a seat in the last row. But she was no longer the woman that had left this town. Now she was well dressed and groomed and unrecognizable to the locals. When Jack got to her seat she remained looking down and crying into her purse. But Jack didn't give up easily if he thought people were being stingy. He just stood there and breathed a little harder. When she regained her composure she said "we're going to have to get you some onion with a little less aroma." Then she looked up at him but her voice had paralyzed him after a long moment he said "you're her."

"I'm who" she asked?

"The woman in my head" he said.

That got him a kick in the shins and a gentle whisper in his ear that said "I don't know what you do when you're dead but from now on I'd better be the only woman in your head."

She couldn't say any more because he was hugging and kissing her and the congregation was shouting hallelujah. Jack looked down expecting to see a peg but there wasn't one.

"Your leg grew back" he said in amazement.

"No" she said "it's one of those prostitute ones."

"You mean prosthesis" he said kicking her gently in the shin.

"The same thing" she said. "They're both substitutes." The reverend was sure that Jack had really lost it now and was hollering for him to unhand that woman.

Jack hollered back "its okay it's Peggy Sue she didn't know you had exercised me."

"It's exor, Oh Never mind just bring her up here I want to hug her too." When the hugging was all over and the congregation had left she whispered in Jack ear

"I think we should get a motel for the night."

"Why?" Jack asked.

"Because I know why we couldn't have children, but it's all right now and my biological clock says we should get started right away."

Then with a gentle kick in the shins she asked "Why didn't you tell me you were alive?"

"I wasn't" he said "until I saw you again. You were just a vision that kept appearing in my head."

Home Again

The reverend explained that "no one had any idea where you had gone and you didn't answer any of our ads."

When she had a moment alone with the reverend she said "you didn't really exorcise him did you?"

"The Lord works in mysterious ways" he said "and like the Tower of Pisa some times you have to lean to get attention. At least that's according to Dad."

At the motel Peggy Sue told Jack about the woman in the theatre and how she had feared that her children wouldn't love her because she only had one foot. But the woman's children had shown her that if you loved them enough nothing else mattered.

Peggy Sue was so serious about having children that she started off with twins, one of each! Jack claimed he had arranged it that way to keep the tradition in the family. Peggy Sue made him swear in front of the reverend that he would never wrestle alligators again. He got enough wrestling with Peggy Sue and the kids. They kept the house in New York City for business reasons and contact with Sarah and Sickle. In the spring they would move Ali back to the park where he was once again a star.

Jack was so fascinated by his children he spent many hours watching them and studying every feature of their face. As their daughter grew he began to notice a difference in her that hadn't been obvious to him before. Her hair was blacker and her lips were thicker than any of the rest of the family. She also seemed to tan a lot faster and maintain it longer. Troubled and unwanted thoughts began to form in Jacks head.

Could it be that Peggy Sue had had a lover when they were separated? Possibly Negroid or Asian. Could it also mean that she was already pregnant when she appeared at the reverends meeting and fulfilled his life once again?

He loved his children and there was no way in the world that he could live without them. He became frustrated and angry. His disposition began to take its toll on his and Peggy Sue's relation ship, which had been an example to all their friends. Jack was considering going to New York and searching out this man when Sickle the only friend he confided in came for a visit and noticed right away that something was not right with his friend.

What is biting your butt he asked him and don't tell me nothing?

Have you noticed anything unusual about my daughter Jack asked?

No! Sickle said. She's a mulatto beauty just like your momma.

My mom was a mulatto Jack said throwing his arm around him and kissing him on the cheek.

What the hell is the mater with you Sickle asked? Get out of my face. That gator must have dropped you on your head.

I love you Jack said just live with it! I've got to go and make sure some one else knows I love her.

The compromise

Leo had finally found Rhonda and brought her back as his wife. His disappointment at the turn of events was obvious. Jack though had been giving it a lot of thought and Max., Tilley and Ti were due to come for a summer visit. That would be a good time to lay his idea on them. He had already tested it out on Peggy Sue. Who was interested but wanted feed back from more knowledgeable people. When they arrived and had settled in Jack called for a round table discussion about the equipment that was laying on the property and what should be done with it. The reverend was also asked to sit in due to his standing in the neighbor hood. Max and Tilley being the rightful owner were the first to be asked if they had any plans for it. Max informed them that he had inquired about selling it and had received no bites at all. It was obvious that all of the old circus crowed were aging and content with their lives as is. He claimed he would be happy to hear anyone's input on the matter. That statement opened the gate for Jack to introduce his idea. We have been endowed with a hundred acres of land here by the minister Richard Blessing. Who out of the goodness of his heart has given both Derrick and my self his good name. On top of that we have quite a collection of circus apparatus belonging to Max. It is not enough to build a circus but enough to make an amusement park and Flea market with a merry go round. Leo broke the silence with how about a petting zoo? You know with animals that are cute and cuddly and eat hay instead of people. My wife says she'll kill me if I get eaten by the performers. Rhonda and I were thinking of buying a house near here and we could be here year round. Since we would only have to open in the summer and on special occasions. Jack suggested, we could cut you out a few acres and help you build a house to blend in with the theme. We could do the same for the reverend and build a church. We could also make the park a corporation and allot shares for labor. The concept had caught fire now and the ideas would rival Wonder land.

They found Ali lying dead on the beach one morning after a particularly busy week end. It would seem someone had thrown or dropped a case of beer in the pond and Ali had eaten the whole thing in his glutinous manner. Whether or not the contents had killed the pain we'll never know but there was little sign of thrashing around on the beach. It was suggested to Peggy Sue frequently that she should make accessories such as hand bags and shoes out of him since his hide was such an unusual color. Peggy Sue could in no way contemplate such an idea. For good and bad Ali had been a main player in their lives and as such deserved to be buried in the family plot with full honors. Every year on the anniversary of his death the fast growing congregation would gather at the pond and pay him tribute by throwing onions in the water around a water spouting statue of Ali.

In time all the plans they had made came to be and they dwelt in the Max & Blessing Park with their ever growing families. No needy person ever left the property hungry or broke.

Jack outlived all his peers and was buried with Peggy Sue next to Ali who had in an unorthodox way been both their nemesis and mentor through this life.

The End